The Adventures of
Wilder Good

THE
ADVENTURES
OF

#4

The Adventures of
Wilder Good

THE GREEN COLT

S. J. DAHLSTROM

Illustrations by Cliff Wilke

PAUL DRY BOOKS
Philadelphia   2016

First Paul Dry Books Edition, 2016

Paul Dry Books, Inc.
Philadelphia, Pennsylvania
www.pauldrybooks.com

Printed in the United States of America

CIP data available at the Library of Congress
ISBN-13: 978-1-58988-114-3

for my Dad—
who gave me the durable gifts of nature
and of books.

CONTENTS

Don't give your son money. As far as you can afford it, give him horses. No one ever came to grief—except honourable grief—through riding horses.

WINSTON CHURCHILL
My Early Life

The Texans are perhaps the best at the actual cowboy work. They are absolutely fearless riders and understand well the habits of the half wild cattle . . . while in the use of the rope they are only excelled by the Mexicans.

THEODORE ROOSEVELT
Hunting Trips of a Ranchman

CHAPTER ONE

The Duck
and the Coyote

"Wilder, I want to tell you a story," Papa Milam said to his grandson sitting next to him.

The pair sat and stared into the black night of the grass trap pasture, their legs dangling off the pickup bed into the dark that surrounded them. They were almost invisible to each other, just two voices surrounded by silence. They were stiff and sore, hands swollen and puffy like winter wool gloves from the digging. Wilder's body felt like a wrecked car, but his mind was sharp.

"When I came back from the war in Europe my thoughts were all twisted around—like when a barbed-wire fence is stretched real tight. And then a bull or something runs through it, and the tension breaks and it snaps and the wire wraps all around itself and everything and gets all twisted up in a big knot.

"Well, I was back here at the ranch and it had been dry for a long time, like it is now, and all I did was work every day for Dad. I didn't hunt or fish or go to town. I just worked. That next spring a big rain came and broke the drought, and it must have rained about ten inches on the dry ground in a few days. All the ponds and cow tanks filled up and overflowed, and it kind of lifted me a little.

"In that big tank in the Lower Upton pasture, I noticed a pair of mallard ducks one day. They don't usually stop here to nest, but every day I saw them there. I got to where I would go and check on them and throw chicken scratch out onto the water. They never came close to me, but when I would go back a ways in the pasture they would come and eat the corn or milo.

"One day the green-headed drake was gone, and I knew that meant the hen had set up shop with a nest of eggs. She was on her own out here in the wilderness, and I felt scared for her because I had really come to like seeing them and I think it gave me hope for the first time. I didn't look for the nest in the bunch grass and mesquites around the pond, but I figured it was close. I started carrying my rifle, the .270 I gave you, in the pickup so I could shoot any coyotes or coons or whatever I might happen to see looking for those eggs as well. But it had quit raining and the pond was going down faster than I expected it to. The ground sucked the water up faster than usual since it had been completely dry before that big rain. I gathered all the cattle in the pasture and moved them to the Mesa pasture just to keep the cows out of the water and away from that nest of eggs. Dad said that was silly, to shut down a pasture for a nest of duck eggs, but he went along with it.

"And then one day it happened—there was a line of six fuzzy tiny ducks out there in the tank behind that little hen. I guess I had seen ducks all my life but never really noticed them before. She was as brave and true as any mother I have ever seen, human or animal. Together they seemed like the prettiest things in all creation, and even though I hadn't done anything really, I was as proud of them as I was of every cow and horse on the place. I can't explain it, but I was.

"But the pond was shrinking. Fast. I looked up in an encyclopedia at the house that mallards need five to six weeks before they can fly. I didn't think they were going to make it, but there wasn't anything for me to do. I got to watching them every day. I would sit about 50 yards off at the corner of the dam and watch them feed and swim and talk to their mother. She would do a little whisper call when a hawk or falcon came by overhead, and then they all swam like little motor boats to the shade of that big native elm that grows on the north side. The one that is still there.

"I realized one day that I wasn't the only one watching the shrinking pond and the growing ducks. A coyote was too. I first saw her sitting under that elm, sitting straight up on her rump like a dog with its ears up, just watching those ducks. It was a female and she had a thinning spring coat that was real dark. Not black like wolf, but darker than most coyotes. I thought to shoot her at first, but I couldn't bring myself to shoot a gun, and especially not at a living thing. I had been raised with it, but since the war I had had enough. So I would throw rocks at her and scare her off.

"Each day I watched the pond shrink, and most days I saw the coyote or its tracks circling the pond. It made my stomach sick. I watched and hoped and prayed for rain like I never had before. The hen and those chicks just needed a few more weeks and they could be gone and safe.

"But it never rained. The pond wasn't 20 feet across now, maybe two feet deep in the middle. I hadn't seen the coyote for a few days, and kept my fingers crossed.

"It was just into July and it was about 100 degrees, and I went to check my ducks around lunchtime and the pond was clear of ducks. It wasn't much more than a big mud puddle now.

My heart sank into my stomach. As I circled the pond, coming close for the first time in weeks, I saw something move under the black shade of the elm. It was the dark female coyote. She began to move off from me, but she moved slow and was only about 30 yards from me when I saw her. It looked like something was wrong with her.

"When she got out from under the tree I knew what it was. She was bloated from gorging herself on my ducks. Our eyes locked and she looked like a scolded pup. There was a pile of feathers at my feet, and I saw the hen's long brown wing feathers in the mess. That coyote had waited until the pond was gone, watching just like me, and then she butchered every single duck during the night. That fine little hen could have flown away, but she stayed and fought to the death for her young.

"Well, I saw red and knew I would have my vengeance. It was just like the war again. I sprinted to the pickup that was back behind the dam. I started the truck and raced to the top side of the pond where I knew I could cover the coyote's retreat. I saw her trying to lope off, but she was slow and I knew I would take her easily. Her abdomen swollen from the feast, she now looked more like an old cow carrying twins than a sleek-coated coyote. I grabbed the .270 and jacked in a shell and laid the rifle across the red hot hood of the pickup. My skin sizzled but I didn't mind as I found my rest and gathered the dog in my crosshairs.

"I can still see it in slow motion. She was about 150 yards out in the sand sage, and I picked a window and fired. The bullet made a little poof when it hit her in the flank, and she snapped back at the wound with her mouth as the slug simultaneously spun her around and laid her on the ground for the last time. I shot her again to make sure.

"I drove up to her with my heart racing as if it was the first thing I had ever killed. She was a mess from the two big rounds. She was dead. I threw her in the pickup bed and drove to the south fence line that faces the river and tied her upside down by the feet on the top wire of the barbed-wire fence as a warning to other coyotes."

Papa paused. He shifted his seat on the hard steel pickup bed. Wilder gulped but didn't look up at him. After a minute Papa continued, "Wilder, I've had 50 years to think about that. But now I want to ask you, who was in the wrong, me or the coyote?"

CHAPTER TWO
Back in Texas

Twelve-year-old Wilder Good sat on the long front porch of his granddad's house and watched the bees buzzing in the bluebonnets next to the steps. His granddad, Papa Milam, was gone somewhere in his pickup and trailer into the dusty drought of the ranch. It wasn't a bad drought yet, Papa said, but only getting an inch in May and seventy-hundredths in June was a poor start to the spring.

Papa's dog, Coffee, sat stately in Wilder's lap. The blue heeler seemed glad to have Wilder back in Texas. But it was already too hot to have a dog in his lap even though it was only mid-June. Wilder shoved her off and lay down on the porch to get a better look at the bees.

He took off his hat and stretched on his belly, chin on his hands, and stared at the delicate blue flowers. They really did look like old-time sun bonnets when he was up close. The bees methodically seemed to hit each bloom up and down the tall lupine spikes. They drank nectar from each bonnet and packed bright orange bundles of pollen on their back legs to carry back to their hive. Wilder assumed they were honey bees and wished he knew where their hive was, not that he had any idea of how to steal their honey. But it was a fine thought to him, harvesting a little wildflower honey. It would be the mountain man thing to do.

Suddenly Coffee shot off the porch like a rocket, which wasn't unusual. The protective blue heeler often did that when she smelled a coyote on the breeze. After a few seconds Wilder glanced up in the dog's direction to see the horses running toward the pens like a waterfall down from the Upper Upton pasture.

The grass trap gates were open, and although Wilder was probably a hundred yards away, he heard the thunder of nine horses on open ground and it made his heart beat faster. They stopped at the water trough, snorting and kicking and jumping, feigning indignation at being caught. Right behind them came Papa loping his gray gelding, Atticus. He was wearing a white long-sleeve pearl-snap shirt like always, with Levi's and his shotgun chaps. Like Wilder, he wore a gray felt Stetson, only his had wispy gray hairs sticking out underneath. Coffee had joined the old man on his right side and was aiming aggressive but gutless barks toward the horses. The dog stayed close to Papa in the off-center dogtrot that only heelers can do, looking like her back legs were going to overrun the front.

Wilder stood up and put his hat on and walked out to Papa.

Papa, still in the saddle, had parked Atticus next to the six-board-high wood fence of the corrals. Wilder could see that he wanted him to climb up and be on eye level with him. He was 75 years old but horses running wild still fired up Papa. He sat there admiring them, almost forgetting what he was doing in the first place. Wilder broke the silence from atop the fence.

"Pretty horses, Papa."

"Yes they are, Wilder. I sure love 'em." He sat straight, both hands on the saddle horn, the split leather reins feathered neatly between the first three fingers of his right hand.

"Are we doing something with them today? Should I get my gear?"

"Wilder, you're a good rider and a good hand. I don't worry much when you are with me." He paused and rubbed his clean-shaven jaw. Wilder listened, embarrassed by the compliment, and looked at the horses, all taking deep-sucking drinks at the trough.

"But almost all your horse and cow work

has been on Fancy or other broke-to-death horses. You don't really know what you know, yet—if that makes any sense. A lot of cowboys look good on good horses, but that's 95 percent horse and 5 percent rider. I want you to really *know* horses.

"What you need is a green colt, a horse to work with that doesn't know any more than you do. That is the only way to learn. Train one from the ground up, and figure it out for yourself."

Papa kept his eye on the horses milling around the corral. Wilder nodded at the announcement.

"A horse is kind of like a whetstone. You can pull a knife across a whetstone all day if you want, but the blade will only be as sharp or as dull as your ability to hold a consistent angle. When you start a colt, it can only be as good a horse as you are a teacher. A horse is a reflection of the man that rides him. Nothing more."

Wilder felt a rush of excitement at Papa's words, but the feeling didn't stay long—about a second. The sinking feeling of fear replaced it as he considered the reels of memory he had of rough horses bucking men off and the wrecks he had heard stories of his whole life. They were glamorous as he saw them from a distance, but thinking about himself actually breaking a colt was another thing. He knew it was dangerous; he knew it was work.

"Your parents only wanted to drop you off for the weekend, but I asked them to leave you for a couple of weeks. I may not win that fight, but I think I got at least a few extra days out of them. I'm giving you that blue roan colt over there."

Wilder was speechless. He looked and found the blue roan. He had a black face that faded into a steel blue from the speckling of white hairs, which covered a black skin. It was a horse he had seen the last couple of years in the remuda but had never thought much about. He knew Fancy had foaled a few years ago and this must be him. His nose was down sniffing the ground trying to stay invisible and away from the older and bigger horses.

"He's two, and has never been touched, except for the vet gelding him a few months ago. He is in good flesh this spring, and healthy and strong. Fancy's last foal . . . she is too old now, so I didn't breed her back after this one. I weaned him last year when he was one.

"I'll leave him up this evening, and you can start making friends. Learn as you go."

Papa didn't wait to be thanked. He didn't know if he would be thanked, not because he took Wilder for a brat, but he had some idea what kind of bomb he had just dropped on the unsuspecting boy. He smiled as he rode back out of the grass trap to his pickup and trailer parked at the back end of the pasture.

Wilder only realized he had left after he was 20 yards away. He figured he should say something.

The boy cupped his hands and yelled into the north breeze, "Thanks Papa!" Papa heard him but kept riding. He nodded to himself.

"Does he have a name?" Wilder yelled even louder.

"Not yet," Papa hollered back.

ᗢ

CHAPTER TIIREE

Bluebonnets

Wilder watched the horses for a long time in the shade of the massive cotton-wood trees that grew among the corrals and barns and ranch house. The shallow ground-water that had nourished them for hundreds of years since the place was a buffalo wallow still watered their roots. An hour later when Papa parked his truck in front of the house and walked inside, Wilder left his perch over the horses and headed in, too.

He had tried to entice his horse, in his mind calling him "my horse" for the first time, with a handful of buffalo grass by offering it through the fence. The colt didn't notice. Fancy had come over and gobbled the grass.

At the house he asked, "Papa, can I call Mom and Dad and tell them?"

"Sure," Papa replied from his easy chair.

Wilder dialed the number on the yellowed rotary phone that hung on the kitchen wall. It was dusty on top and had rose-colored makeup residue on the mouthpiece, which smelled like a grandma. The patina of good years that didn't wash off easily. Taped on the wall next to the phone was a list of phone numbers. He saw his home number at the beginning of the list, and a heart next to it in blue ink. At the top of the page of perfect script handwriting it read "Mr. & Mrs. W. E. Milam," and then listed the home number of the ranch. Wilder figured this was his grandma's doing, even though he barely remembered her. He liked the smell of the phone.

On the side of the fridge across from the phone was a faded poster of George Strait. A small calendar at the top left read "1992" but didn't have any writing or marks on it. George looked the same as he always had, Wilder thought, grinning in starched Wrangler jeans. He guessed his grandma had looked at it while she talked on the phone, which was funny to him.

The phone rang twice and seemed to have been picked up with a crash, followed by a bubbly, "Hello, who is it?" Wilder rolled his eyes from his concealment 400 miles away.

Molly.

"It's your awesome brother," Wilder said.

"I'm sorry but I don't have an awesome brother. You must have the wrong number."

"Flopsy, just put on Mom or Dad."

"Wilder, I have a joke."

"I'm busy . . . doing cowboy stuff with Papa."

"Will you forget me in an hour?"

"What?"

"Will you forget me in an hour?"

"I'd like to."

"Wilder, just answer the question, or you can't talk to Mom or Dad."

"OK. No, I won't forget you in an hour."

"Will you forget about me in a day?"

"No."

"Will you forget about me in a week?"

"What is the point of this, Molly?"

"Will you?"

"No," Wilder growled.

"Will you forget about me in a year?"

"No."

"Knock, knock."

"Knock, knock?"

"Yes, Knock, knock," Molly giggled.

"Who's there?"

"YOU FORGOT ABOUT ME!" Molly yelled into the phone, riddled with laughter.

Wilder smiled, realizing against his will that that was a pretty good one. He held the phone down smothering the mouthpiece with his hand and looking around as if someone else could have heard that.

"Haha, I got you," Molly said.

Wilder gave her the moment. He liked his sister, not that he would ever tell her that.

"OK, put Mom on."

"She's not here."

"Yeah right. She wouldn't leave a nine-year-old bozo alone."

"Dad's at work somewhere. Mom is in the garden. The beans are up. Did you know that?"

Exasperated, Wilder gave up. "Molly, just tell Mom and Dad that Papa gave me a horse and that it's OK if I stay here awhile."

Molly didn't seem impressed with the information, but she said OK and they chatted a bit more about the chickens and about what Huck, their dog, was doing in the backyard and what Coffee, Papa's dog, was doing at the ranch. But pretty soon Wilder got nervous about talking too long and making Papa upset. Papa was raised in a time when long-distance phone calls were a luxury, not an everyday occurrence. Papa never said anything about phone calls or saving money exactly, and he had plenty of money at this point in his life, but some things become so ingrained that they stay around long after they make any sense. Wilder knew this and didn't push it. He said goodbye and hung up, trusting Molly to pass on his message to their parents, Hank and Livy.

Wilder wandered into the living room and found Papa asleep in his big chair with his mouth open. Papa always grabbed a 30-minute siesta after lunch. It was kind of spooky actually, because the gray-haired old man looked kind of dead. Wilder knew he wasn't, because dead people didn't snore, but he was sprawled out with his boots off and brown socks showing and the soft padded leather chair in the reclined position. Wilder tiptoed over to the couch that faced the big porch window and lay down.

He didn't sleep; his mind was too busy mulling over names for his horse. Names were important. Wilder had always wanted a horse with an Indian name. Comanche seemed like the first obvious choice. It was an awesome name he thought, but it also seemed like he had known lots of horses with that name. Quanah Parker, Tomahawk, Old Chief, Warclub, Scalper (he liked Scalper a lot), Little Squaw, Wapiti, Pinto, Arrowhead, Spirit Horse . . . his mind ran through all the Indian lore and history that he had tried to accumulate by age twelve. Nothing grabbed him.

Then he saw the bees in the bluebonnets again, through the window. He got up from the couch and went out the front door hoping not to wake Papa. But he was awake already and followed Wilder out the front door a few minutes later with a stack of mail that had collected over several days. Wilder lay down on the porch again, belly down, while Papa sat on a 30-foot-long bench that was actually a faded yellow church pew. He cradled the mail in his lap and flicked through the envelopes one by one.

"Papa, where did all these bluebonnets come from? They don't grow anywhere else on the ranch that I have seen."

Papa didn't look up from the mail. "Your grandmother."

"Grandma liked wildflowers?"

"Yes, she did," he smiled. "She once bought a 50-pound sack of bluebonnet seed. Do you know how much 50 pounds of bluebonnets cost? A lot. Over 300 dollars. She spread them all over the ranch, but they only really took up here at the house. I see them in the pastures from time to time."

"I like them, too." And right then the name for his horse popped into his head. He was a blue roan. His name would be Bluebonnet.

"That's the name then Papa, Bluebonnet."

"The name for what?" Papa looked down at Wilder.

"The colt you gave me. His name is Bluebonnet."

Papa looked off the porch into the distance. After a few seconds he nodded his head and went back to the mail.

"Papa, do you have any paper?"

"What kind of paper?" he looked down at Wilder again. He wasn't annoyed, he loved his grandson, he just wasn't used to so much talking. Talking that always started with "Papa" and was followed by a question.

"Oh, a bunch of printer paper."

"I don't have a printer. Heidi at the bank will make copies for you though," he added, thinking he was helping.

"Do you have any notebooks or writing paper?"

"I can look around. I am sure your grandmother has some somewhere."

Wilder looked at the stack of mail that was now sitting on the pew next to Papa. There had been a small package in it that Papa had opened, and it held a little booklet.

"What's that little booklet you got in the mail?"

Papa looked over, surprised, and picked it up. "It's a tally book from the feed store."

"Do you need it?"

"No, they send one or two every year to thank me for buying my cow cake from them." It still didn't occur to him to offer it to Wilder.

"Can I have it?"

"Sure." He tossed the little book to Wilder on the porch floor. Wilder sat up cross-legged and thumbed the pages. On the front it said "Buzz's Feed and Seed and Saddle Shop." It had about 40 pages and was two inches wide by four inches tall. It was designed to be carried in a front shirt pocket so it could be accessed on horseback when counting cattle. It was small enough to be written on with only a saddle horn for a desk.

It was perfect for Wilder's purpose.

June 15

Papa gave me a horse today. ~~H~~ He is my first horse. He is a blue roan gelding (2 years). His name is Bluebonnet. I will start breaking him tomorrow. Bluebonnet seems like a girl's name but it seems to fit and I think it reminds Papa of Grandma which is good.

I picked out a halter and lead in the barn which Papa said was OK to keep just for my horse.

CHAPTER FOUR
First Touch

On Saturday evening Papa didn't seem to have much to do after he and Wilder cut Bluebonnet out from the other horses. They turned the rest of the remuda loose into the horse pasture. The horse pasture covered at least two sections so they ran off over a canyon like wild mustangs from generations past, while Bluebonnet whinnied and stomped in the corral at being left behind. Horses are intensely communal, and being left alone from the herd inspired a type of panic in the colt. But it was natural, and good for him even, especially with the education he was about to be put through. Isolation would encourage the horse to bond with Wilder, hopefully.

It had been a year since Bluebonnet had been weaned from Fancy, and she didn't respond to his horse talk anymore. He was just another horse now. In fact, sometimes she kicked and bit him pretty hard to remind him of his place in the herd and that while her flank had once meant life-giving milk to the young horse, it now only represented a place of danger. The old mare's rear hooves were ready if he prowled too close to the tender flap of skin that stretched between her belly and thigh.

There was still a little light in the sky after a dinner of leftovers. Saturday was the last night before Papa's cook, Marisol, showed up with a week's worth of food. Wilder had eaten beans and tortillas with salsa on the top—after sniffing several plastic containers full of food. Marisol's cooking was great . . . when he could make out what it was. He knew there was no telling what Papa might have in a container, so he usually ate beans by default. They had each sniffed around and fixed their own meal as they wanted it. This was the accepted rule at the ranch—two bachelors fending for themselves in most everything. Adjusting to the new eating routine away from his mother's food always signaled an abrupt end to his Colorado life.

Wilder walked out to the pen and climbed inside. He didn't fear the colt but knew enough to stay close to a fence and away from its hind end. At dusk the heavy cottonwood trees shaded almost all of the large square pen, which had a water tank sitting in the middle of it, 15 feet in diameter. The stock tank was cut in half by the wooden pen fence that went up and over it. The trees were letting loose a haze of cotton in their attempt to procreate during another spring. Caught by the light of the setting sun, the airy seeds floated like a mass of tiny jellyfish. It looked like the ranch was getting a snow in June.

The tank in the pen was the central and original livestock tank on the ranch from the early 1900s. It was built of stone covered with cement for a stucco seal that was painted white. The tank was fed by a well pumped by a windmill standing next to it. The well was the first on the place and was only 50 feet deep, the family had always bragged. It had never gone dry, the mill's sucker rod gently moving up and down and hauling the cool water north as the creaky tin wheel turned 20 feet in the sky. Wilder worked out from the tank, dipping his hand in the water as he went, easing toward the colt.

Bluebonnet gave him a sincere look, his head up and both ears forward, but he quickly turned his rear to the boy and walked casually to the nearest corner of the pen. Wilder followed. He had never worked a colt before, and he really didn't know what to do. He thought maybe touching it would be a good first move.

But whatever direction Wilder went, the colt moved off, and always with his tail to him. That meant that even in a corner Wilder couldn't get closer than about ten feet. He moved slow and didn't speak. He didn't give in to chasing the colt, but after five minutes of this routine he figured out that it wasn't working.

He jumped the fence and ran inside, past Papa who was on the porch reading a book. He knew it was OK to try and figure this out on his own, so he didn't stop to ask Papa about his new plan. That was the way he had always been taught—figure it out. And propping up that rule were the three West Texas Nevers: never call for help, never ask questions, and never complain.

He burst back out of the house, letting the screen door slam. Papa looked up and saw that Wilder was carrying something in his hands, but he couldn't tell what it was.

Wilder crawled back into the pen and continued his routine of tracking the colt around, but this time he carried an overflowing handful of sugar cubes. He held them out in front of his body with one hand and said, "Here, Blue-bonnet," kind of like calling a cat with a "here kitty-kitty" cadence. Wilder knew it sounded silly, but he didn't know what else to do.

Bluebonnet took notice and let Wilder walk a bit closer this time, deciding to stand and face him. At ten feet, Wilder kept advancing until Bluebonnet spun and went back to the corner, still watching over his shoulder and guarding himself with those powerful hind legs.

Wilder only chased him about a minute this time before giving up. Then he went over to the water tank and sat down, leaning his back against the cool cement wall. He cupped the sugar cubes in his hands and rested them in his lap. He didn't really have any other ideas for what to try next, but he liked being out there, being with his horse, and for the time he was content. He was also exhausted from the long hot day; and it always took a while to adjust to ranch life with Papa—in a wilderness where no mothers lived.

The next thing he knew, he woke up in the dark and his skin felt cold . . . and he was eyeball to eyeball with Bluebonnet. A massive horsehead was nosing around in his lap.

Wilder had always been good at keeping still in tight spots, and he controlled himself this time too, as he roused from his brief nap. He remained frozen in his slumped position, but cracked both eyes. The blue roan colt with his almost completely black head seemed like a ghost in front of him. It was fascinating that this powerful and untouchable animal was inches from him in the murky night. Wilder could smell him for the first time, the wet wildness of horse flesh and the puffs of huge lungs blowing hot air against his belly.

Bluebonnet slobbered and searched the boy's limp hands and jeans and white Wrangler shirt for every morsel of sugar he could find. The colt had never tasted sugar before, but he developed an appreciation very quickly. A minute passed, and the hard, grainy crunching of cubes in giant molars ended. Wilder knew this little visit was coming to an end.

He reached up with his right hand, which had been by the side of his lap, and stroked Bluebonnet on his big left cheek. He said, "Whoa, boy."

Faster than Wilder could realize, the colt snorted and spun, throwing dust all over him. He braced for a defensive kick ... but none came. When Wilder opened his eyes again Bluebonnet was across the pen prancing back and forth with his tail up, snorting and bucking in small jumps.

Wilder stood up and smiled, relieved that he was alive. The sugar was gone, and he had touched his horse. The first step was accomplished. Well done, he thought. He climbed out of the pen and walked to the house.

Papa was still in his chair, with his boots and socks off.

"Papa, I just touched Bluebonnet for the first time. I took some sug—"

Papa cut him off, gently, with a nod. "I know, I watched you. You were thinking right. If something doesn't work, stop, and try something else. I want you to do this on your own, and I believe you will figure it out without a lot of talking from me.

"But, don't give a horse treats, ever. Especially not a colt. That will make him mean and dangerous and he will only do what you ask if you give him something. That's not what you want . . . a pet horse. A horse is not a pet. You want a horse to accept you as master and then to become your partner. It has to be a 50-50 deal."

Wilder looked down, puzzled. He had never heard that before, and it wounded his pride a little. He trusted Papa and wanted to please him more than anything in the world.

"Your mother called and wants us to be at church in the morning," Papa said, moving on. "So, put on the best clothes that you brought and we'll go."

Wilder said a humble "Yes sir" and went to his room. Coffee trotted behind him on her stubby legs. Before shutting his eyes Wilder made another note in his tally book.

June 15 (second entry)
   Don't give treats to horses. Horses are not pets.

CHAPTER FIVE

Churches

The next morning Papa and Wilder drove Grandma's black Cadillac to church in Verbena. The cushy leather seats and the windows rolled up and the air conditioner blasting was all such a different experience than Papa's dusty pickup. The big car took the rutted ranch roads and the 12 cattle guards that connected the ranch to the county highway in big rocking movements as the luxury suspension fought to balance the rough landscape. Instead of a jack hammer ride in a one-ton pickup, it was more of a sailing motion, like they were riding a yacht through a sea of green grass.

Papa's large leather-bound King James Bible rode along with them on the middle seat. Wilder used to sit in that middle seat when he was little, between Papa and Grandma. He remembered that about Grandma.

Wilder didn't know which church they were going to because Papa didn't generally go to church after Grandma died. Her name was Marian, and Wilder remembered a gentle white-haired woman who oversaw his baths as a child. She would wrap him in a towel and pretend he was a package being sent to his grandparents on a train. Then she would slowly open the towel piece by piece and act like it was the biggest thrill in the world to receive a package that turned out to be her grandson.

Papa and Grandma always went to the Methodist church in Verbena, and that was where her funeral had been, Wilder remembered. So he was surprised when Papa pulled up to a much smaller white stucco building with a sign that read "church of Christ meets here." The white caliche parking lot was full, though there were only about 15 vehicles. The "c" in church was purposefully left lower case in the cursive steel sign.

"I guess we're late," Papa said even though he hadn't had any idea what time the service started.

"Why are we at this church?" Wilder asked.

"Isn't this where you go?"

"Uhhh, yes, in Cottonwood. But it doesn't matter where we go today."

"Your mom wanted you to know some of the church of Christ folks in Verbena, she said."

"OK," Wilder replied. He didn't know or remember anybody at either church in Verbena so it didn't bother him either way. He knew the Methodists did some different things, but he didn't really know enough about it for it to matter to him.

As they walked into the humble building, Papa and Wilder took off their hats and laid them upside down on the double shelf that hung over the coat rack. There weren't any coats or umbrellas on the rack, but there were about 10 hats next to theirs, straws and felts, all laid upside down. Most were Sunday hats and showed no signs of sweat or stain, whereas Papa's and Wilder's were their normal everyday hats and were pretty covered in dark stains that littered the gray felt. Wilder's hatband held his "Hall of Fame" collection of fishing flies.

A man about Papa's age came out of the main auditorium, which they could see from the lobby through the glass windows on the double doors. He had a big smile and big ears next to a close-cropped white stubble haircut. Behind both ears he wore large flesh-toned hearing aids. When the doors shut behind him from the Bible class in progress he said to Papa, "Hello, Wendell!"

"Hello, Clarence," Papa replied with a matching smile.

"This must be your grandson?" He extended his large right hand to Wilder after shaking Papa's hand. Wilder nodded and took it, giving him a strong shake in return.

"I am Wilder Good, sir."

"And my name is Clarence Thames." His eyes beamed down on Wilder, but it was his ears that sent the strongest message. They wiggled . . . quite a lot. Wilder turned his head a bit, like a dog, to refocus on the strange sight. Clarence could wiggle his ears like a rabbit, and he enjoyed showing the talent off to kids.

Clarence laughed and tousled Wilder's hair with his whole palm, messing up his hair, which he had combed with his fingers and a splash of water. Wilder was a little annoyed at the gesture, but knew it was meant as a sign of acceptance. The gentle hair rubbing reminded him of Bluebonnet fishing around in his lap for the sugar cubes last night. Touch was friendly, an absence of fear, he figured. He wondered what his horse was doing and felt like he was losing time with him.

Clarence was the preacher at the church, as well as a farmer and rancher. The preaching wasn't a salaried position. His hearing had gradually left him after initial damage as an MP in WWII and then 50 years of driving a tractor before enclosed cabs were invented and then afforded. Clarence had been the mayor, school board president, a volunteer firefighter, and just about everything else in the community. He was universally loved and respected across Roosevelt County, but he wasn't a small-town politician out to get a favor or a check.

Clarence was just a gentle man. Papa had known him his whole life, like most of the people in the county.

He didn't quiz Papa about why they were there this Sunday morning or any other church-related things. He shifted his weight to one leg and faced the auditorium, the same direction as Papa, and the two men discussed the weather and grass and planting and the early hot spell they were in. Clarence told Papa that he always prayed for Livy and asked how she was. Livy was Papa's daughter and Wilder's mother who had breast cancer. Livy had been raised in the Verbena community and they hadn't forgotten. They talked for ten minutes and Clarence didn't act like there was anything else they needed to be doing, like getting into Bible class.

Finally Papa offered, "You want us to get into class?" Papa knew the church of Christ folks had Bible class for a full hour *before* the hour-and-a-half service. All that church made his head swim and was probably the reason they had stayed Methodists all those years. But he liked the church of Christ folks as well as anyone.

"Sure. Wilder, do you want to come in with Wendell and me to the adult class? There's also a class for your age right here." Clarence asked this in a man's voice. He wasn't speaking down to Wilder in offering the option.

Wilder wasn't scared of new people, so he said his age would be fine, and Clarence walked him into the small room to the right and introduced him. Wilder saw right off the class wasn't really his age. An older lady with gray hair was seated in the middle of a room with nine kids, ages eight to about fifteen Wilder guessed. The youngest, a boy, was picking his nose. The teacher stopped the lesson and asked Wilder about himself, and he replied with sincere answers, if brief. He was the only one without a Bible, which kind of embarrassed him, which the teacher, Mrs. Hill, observed and remedied.

The lesson was the parable of the Prodigal Son. Wilder figured he knew that one pretty well, but he kept any insights to himself. He couldn't understand anybody raising pigs, much less eating their food.

Thirty minutes later there was a knock on the door and the class wrapped up. Wilder left the room with the other kids and sat down next to Papa on the second to last pew. There were only about ten pews per row and three rows across, so no matter where you sat, you were still pretty close to the front.

A podium in the front and center of the sanctuary stood on a raised wooden area that rested on a tan asbestos tile floor. The pews were wood too, no cushions, with the exception of several old corduroy pillows lying here and there. They must have served to offset the circulation problems that bottoms developed during the long services. Behind the podium was a baptistry, which looked kind of like a dark square cave, and on the back wall behind it was hand-painted a lush mountain scene with tropical plants and white-capped mountains. To the right of the podium hung a sign with six rows for number cards to be slid in and out of. It kept track of attendance for Bible class, Sunday service, and Wednesday service. It also recorded the monthly budget and the week's giving. The Sunday service numbers had just been updated to 47. Bible class had been 27.

After the opening prayer, two Mexican men walked in quietly from the back while the song leader announced the first song number. Both men had light tan foreheads and sweat ring indentions around their heads from wearing cowboy hats, the same as Papa. They sat at the other end of the pew from Papa and Wilder. Wilder saw right off that one of them was Artemio Leal, a good friend of Papa's who worked on the neighboring ranch for Papa's buddy, Red Guffey.

The other man glanced at Wilder and seemed to look right through him. Something about his intense, hollow look intimidated Wilder immediately. When Wilder lowered his eyes, he saw that the man was missing a thumb.

CHAPTER SIX
The Little Tick

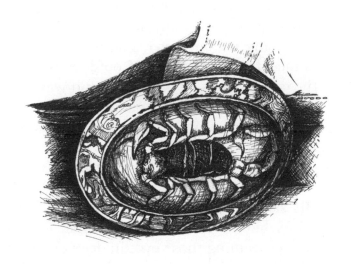

Artemio looked surprised at seeing Papa. But he quickly nodded to him, and a big smile spread across his teeth that seemed to appear whiter than anyone else's. They weren't really any whiter, but his skin was so darkly tanned from a lifetime of outdoor work that the contrast was striking. Artemio was always happy, which seemed to suit his plump belly and friendly eyes. His personality was much like Red's, round and happy.

The man sitting next to Artemio was younger, maybe by 10 years, and looked to be about 50. His skin was weathered and dark like Artemio's, but he had black hawk-like eyes and creases framing those eyes in deep crow's feet. His hair was neatly cut and peppered black and white, mostly white around the ears. He wore a short brown brush jacket that had rips and sewn-up rips all over it. His features looked a bit like Artemio's—high cheek bones, strong chin, and a subtle Roman nose. But he wasn't chubby like Artemio; he had the hardened look of a horseman, no fat anywhere.

Artemio sang pretty well in English, but the other man kept his serious look as he stood and listened. Singing a capella, the congregation kept its beat without a piano or organ, just the rhythmic movement of the song leader's right hand. The thumbless man didn't look uncomfortable, but he didn't try and sing.

Clarence preached from the backside of the front pew which he half-sat on. It was a good sermon, Papa thought, about the glory of God from the book of Job: how God was both rough and gentle from what He described about the animals and creation, and it got to making Papa feel a little guilty about his conversation with Wilder last night. He thought that God was harsh on Job and there Job was just trying to do the best he could. It made Papa feel like Wilder, always these big speeches from people, and just having to suck it up. Papa wasn't used to worrying about other people, or their feelings.

When the sermon, invitation song, collection (Papa slipped a check in, which surprised Wilder), and Lord's Supper and all the other movements of the service were over, including a long and wandering closing prayer that mentioned the drought and rain several times, Papa went over to Artemio. Wilder stood behind him in the pew.

Artemio spoke first, "Buenos dias, Wendell! I'n suprized to see you heer." Artemio spoke a more than serviceable English, although the pronunciation was off. Spanish and English drifted in and out of the both men's conversation like it always had in Texas. That was Spanglish. The amalgam of the two languages was truly a regional dialect that only farmers and ranchers knew.

"Buenos dias para ti, Art," Papa said, his eyes twinkling in acknowledgment of the question, and his pronunciation being equally poor when he spoke Spanish. "Oh, Wilder and I like to get around," Papa answered Art's initial question. Both men knew that was all they would say about the strange church appearance. Papa asked about Artemio's wife, Flora, who was home sick. Then the four shuffled out of the pew knowing the introduction of Artemio's friend was next.

"Quien is tu compadre?" Papa asked.

"Mi compadre? This is mi hermanito, my little brother!" Artemio said excitedly. "Te llamo is Tequito."

Tequito Leal offered his hand and shook with Papa and then Wilder. Wilder and Tequito nodded at each other. His hand was hard and calloused, and it felt more like saddle leather than human skin. Wilder braced himself not to look at the stub of a thumb on his hand. He didn't look down, but he could tell it wasn't there from the shake. In its place was a thick ball of muscle, the lower thumb, which was clearly still functional.

Under his brown brush jacket he wore a crisp-pressed blue denim Wrangler shirt, and it was fastened to the top. The top neckline hole being a button, not a pearl snap. Not many cowboys did that, Wilder knew. Tequito was clean-shaven, and while his eyes were not mean, they were strong and intense like a black rain cloud right before it hits.

Wilder saw that his belt buckle had a scorpion in it. It wasn't an engraving or a picture, it was a real, evil-looking black-and-yellow scorpion encased in some kind of glass or epoxy on a blue mother-of-pearl background. He was pretty sure the scorpion couldn't sting him, but still he didn't want to get too close. Wilder sensed this man was different.

The other members of the small congregation were nonchalantly but purposefully gathering behind Wilder and Papa, wanting to greet the visitors. Artemio, who was a member of the church, noticed and got his lunch invite in, before anybody else could. He asked Papa to meet them at La Hacienda for lunch and Papa accepted.

Artemio was correct about his lunch-invite perception, because several others made the same invite. Clarence and his wife, Letha, invited Papa and Wilder over to their house for lunch, but Papa had to decline. The Bible-class teacher, Mrs. Hill, gave Wilder a big hug before they left and kissed him on the cheek, which left some lipstick on him.

Artemio and Tequito were already sitting at a table at La Hacienda when Papa and Wilder walked in. The restaurant was one long open corridor, a re-purposed general store of some kind. The walls were filled with green-and-red-decorated Mexican sombreros and numerous paintings of bull fighting scenes. Wilder was drawn to one of them, in which the blood falling from the bull's back appeared quite vivid. He reached out and touched it with one finger. It was velvet. Behind the cash register hung a large oil painting of Jesus. It showed His heart outside His chest, flaming, with a ring of thorns around it.

On the drive from church to La Hacienda, Papa had formed a plan to deal with the feelings that the sermon had prompted in him. He had never met Tequito before, but he had heard plenty about him over the years from Artemio. He was about the best *vaquero* and horseman anywhere in Mexico, as Art told it. Vaquero was Spanish, roughly, for cowboy. He had developed quite a name for himself over the years, and ranches in Texas had tried to hire him, but for some reason Tequito always stayed south of the border.

He had acquired his nickname when he was a boy and he had begun climbing up on horses and colts. He had possessed a natural feel for stock and for making them do what he wanted. Nothing could throw him off, and he seemed to have little interest in anything else but riding horses. He was like a tick on a horse's back, seemingly embedded in place. Hence the name in Spanish, Tequito, or little tick. The name was half English and half Spanish, "teq" being a corruption of the English word "tick," and -*ito* was Spanish for little.

Cowboying and ranching were trades where, as Papa had learned them, a man could pretty well be judged at first appearance, by his riding gear and clothes. If a man had spent hours in the saddle, you could just tell by the way he walked, the sweat and crease on his hat, and by the way he looked at you. It was hard to explain, because it never *was* explained, but it was just as plain as if it had been written on a t-shirt that said "Cowboy." (Only, cowboys didn't wear t-shirts, not in public anyway.) Papa could tell Tequito was the real deal.

When Papa and Wilder were seated, Artemio explained right off, "Tequito no habla Englis." Papa nodded at both of them and gave them a smile that said no problem.

"Well, horses and cows don't either," Papa added, and he launched his pitch to try to get Tequito on the ranch for a couple days to show Wilder a few things about breaking colts. He assumed Tequito wouldn't be interested, but he was willing to pay his regular daywork fee and then some. Papa thought it would be good for Wilder to have a break from him, and the boy would be working with a top hand.

Papa explained some of this, but not the part about his having been too abrupt with Wilder the night before. He told Artemio that Wilder was breaking a two-year-old gelding, and he would like Tequito to watch a bit and show Wilder a few things. He didn't want Tequito to do the job for him, or just babysit his grandson, but he would appreciate his being around and passing down a few things. He offered Tequito's normal daywork rate, plus an extra $100 a day, for two or three days.

Wilder didn't know what to think about the

conversation, but he kept quiet. He only under-stood small pieces of it anyway.

Artemio translated the offer to Tequito while Papa and Wilder ordered. The Mexican waitress winked at Papa and asked who Wilder was. She confirmed that he wanted item 6A from the menu, which surprised Wilder again. It was a chile relleno and a red enchilada with guaca-molc. A chile relleno is a green chile pepper stuffed with cheese and deep fried in a light flour batter. Wilder ordered the same thing ex-cept with a green enchilada. Red and grccn were different phases of the same pepper, and either one could be hotter depending on the day. Mainly Wilder was looking forward to the fluffy fried sopapillas and honey at the end of the meal.

After a brief exchange and few looks Wild-er's way, Tequito nodded to his brother. Papa knew it was a done deal and smiled and looked at Tequito, "Soy feliz, compadre. Gracias," he said, which meant "I am happy, friend."

When the chips and salsa showed up Wilder looked at Papa, realizing he knew this little family Mexican restaurant pretty well, "Papa, is their salsa hot?"

"Not to me." He winked at Artemio and Te-quito. "But salsas are like dogs, or horses—

when you meet a new one it's best to be real cautious."

June 16

I fed Bluebonnet grass hay and oats this morning and again tonight. I wasn't able to touch him. He didn't seem to remember I was the guy that gave him sugar cubes.

I took it easy and read some Louis L'Amour to him. I'm not sure if he listened, L'Amour wasn't really a cowboy as far as I can tell. He knew a lot about fighting though.

~~I feel kind of scared.~~

ᴡᴳ

CHAPTER SEVEN
'Mira me'

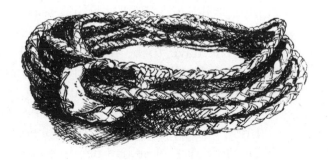

A t the kitchen table the next morning, over fresh Marisol-prepared breakfast burritos, Papa explained to Wilder his arrangement with Tequito. Wilder's initial reaction wasn't excitement. Why did he need help? he thought. And why did it have to be a stranger who didn't even speak English? He kept these questions to himself but hinted at them out loud.

"Papa, aren't we cowboys?" Wilder asked.

"I don't know. Maybe." Papa looked up from the *Livestock Weekly* he had begun to read spread out on the table. "Let others call you that if they want to. Not yourself. That's what I've always thought."

"Well, I mean, do they even cowboy in Mexico?"

Papa's gray and untrimmed eyebrows shot up. "Do they cowboy in Mexico? Wilder, they invented it."

"What do you mean?"

"Texas cowboys may get all the movies and magazines, but we've only been chasing cows for about 150 years. The Mexican vaquero goes back about 400 years. Everything we know we learned from them. We have changed it a bit, but all our gear and most of our language came from them. If it wasn't for them, we'd all be riding flimsy little English saddles no bigger'n a wallet and chasing foxes like George Washington.

"You are getting a chance to work with centuries of tradition today. Tequito isn't some 19-year-old calf roper from Amarillo with a 50-thousand-dollar pickup his dad bought him. And horse someone else trained. He's a man who has started thousands of horses with no cameras around. He's from the state of Jalisco in Old Mexico. Jalisco is kind of like Texas for Mexico. He is what we say . . . *much cowboy.*"

Wilder nodded and ate a bite of biscuit smothered in sandhill plum jelly.

"It's still your job, your colt. But when Tequito wants to show you something, step back and pay attention. It'll be up to you how much you learn."

"But he doesn't even speak English. And I hardly know any Spanish."

"Like I said yesterday, neither do the horses, but they seem to figure it out . . . if they have any brains." He paused and added, "Communication is a lot more than talking."

Wilder felt he had probably said more than he should, so he picked up the breakfast plates and rinsed them in the sink. He gathered up his gear from his room and headed to the pens. He had brought his saddle with him from home—it had been his mother's old saddle, which Papa had given him—as well as all his assorted riding and cowboy gear. He carried it all out to the corral where Bluebonnet waited and hung it up on one of the hitching posts outside the pen.

To his surprise he saw a pickup parked under the cottonwood tree near the pens and Tequito standing there talking to Papa. Tequito nodded as Papa tried to be friendly and get a few words out that might make sense. Tequito was used to the routine and understood a little, but mostly nodded and studied the colt. When Papa saw Wilder rummaging around with his gear he said "Adios" and got in his pickup and drove out past the barns and up toward the Dugout Canyon pasture.

Wilder didn't know what to do. There they were—a colt, a seasoned vaquero, and a kid. All things that he thought he loved, but he felt like he was swimming in the deep end of a pool and the edge was a long way off. He glanced at Tequito.

Tequito relaxed his countenance for the first time since Wilder had seen him, although they didn't make eye contact. He turned and sat down and leaned back on the large cottonwood trunk outside the corral. He was wearing a palm leaf straw hat turned up on the sides pretty dramatically in a "taco" shape. He took off the hat and laid it upside down next to him. He grabbed a tuft of buffalo grass and placed a stem in his mouth like a toothpick.

Wilder turned and climbed into the pen with a halter and lead. If he was going to break Bluebonnet, he needed to catch him, so he figured he needed to get the colt haltered. The boy started off cautious, with respect for Bluebonnet and for his rear hoofs. But the same routine developed as the day before, and the day before that. Bluebonnet walked away and turned his rump. After ten minutes Wilder felt stupid, but he kept his eyes on Tequito and he began to sweat; the day's heat was rising quickly.

Wilder began to twirl the lead in his hand, about four feet of rope, hoping to scare the horse into facing him. Bluebonnet just moved along the square fence line faster. Wilder cornered him by getting closer than he had before, rump still to him, and slapped the colt on the hind quarters with the lead.

Bluebonnet kicked back at him and charged out of the corner, rearing up in a feigned jump when he got to the next corner. Wilder rushed over and slapped him on the rump again. The horse reared and spun off and raised dust all over the pen. Wilder was mad now. No horse was going to tell him what to do.

He smacked the horse on the rump again, even though he knew that wasn't working and that he was just being mean. He threw the halter on the ground and jumped the fence to get the rope off his saddle. "Alright, it's roping time now, colt," Wilder thought to himself.

Back in the pen he swung a large helicopter loop over his head that made the whites show in Bluebonnet's eyes. Wilder rushed in close and threw the loop at the horse. It was a poor shot, and the loop failed to crest the colt's ears, landing roughly on his back and neck. The horse jumped and bucked wildly and ran right past Wilder to the locked gate of the corral. He made a half jump and crashed into the gate. The gate held, and Bluebonnet fell down on his side.

He sprang up, prancing around with his tail twitched up. He snorted around the pen, and soon Wilder had another loop built and was twirling it high above his head in the dust that had filled the air. Another miss and another crash into the gate. Bluebonnet was panicked now. Blood dripped from his head and right front knee. "Well, that's what you get for being stupid," Wilder thought.

Wilder threw another loop, oblivious to everything but catching this horse and showing him who was boss. Bluebonnet had his head over the gate when Wilder threw, and when the hard poly rope struck his head the horse hit the gate with all 900 pounds of wild colt muscle in a frantic jump. His front half cleared the gate but his back half didn't. The colt rocked back and forth on top of the gate like a seesaw, and in a loud crash the gate gave way and the colt went down with it. But then he was up in a wild spin and off at a run to the safety of the grass trap. Chunks of sod flew high over his back.

Wilder gulped and ran to the opened gate in the thick dust. A figure moved to his right, and then a white loop like a huge butterfly floated into the dust and gently fell around the running Bluebonnet's neck like an elegant pearl necklace.

Wilder looked over to see Tequito on the end of a rope. It was a reata, a long rawhide rope that Wilder had seen only in photographs. Tequito had the rope anchored behind the lower half of his rear, with a hand on each side. The 55-foot pasture reata's extra coils lay neatly to his left in the grass. Bluebonnet hit the end of the rope and the loop jerked tight. Tequito never moved.

But he fed a little rope out and it zipped through his hardened hands and across his rear, and Bluebonnet came to a soft and surprising halt, the reata tight around his muscled, bulging neck. The horse looked around and seemed genuinely shocked that he was no longer running flat out to freedom.

Wilder stared at Tequito and then at the colt, and then back to Tequito. Tequito still had the buffalo grass stem in his mouth, but his hat was on. This was the first time Wilder had been close to him. He smelled like fresh tortillas and horses. He looked down at Wilder and took his right thumbless hand off the rope. He pointed into his eyes which were calm and for the first time, kind, Wilder thought. With his first two fingers pointing into his own eyes making a "v" shape he said to the boy,

"Mira me."

CHAPTER EIGHT
'Potro bien'

Wilder knew "mira me" from the Spanish he had learned at school and during basketball practice from teammates and Coach Chavez. He went to school in Colorado with many Mexicans. It meant "watch me," which was pretty close to how it sounded, "mirror me." More than that, the phrase meant "pay attention." He had never given it much thought, but now the words and the presence of Tequito next to him, anchoring a spooked colt without breaking a sweat, relaxed him. It immediately made him feel strong—being in a dusty pen with a mysterious vaquero working a colt.

The presence of Tequito had caught Bluebonnet's attention too, in more ways than one. The pressure of the rope around his neck had forced the colt to turn towards them. It made a rigid line between man and animal. As soon as the colt pointed his ears up and stood quietly, Tequito let the rope sag a bit, releasing the pressure. Blood and oxygen once again raced through the colt's neck.

Then Tequito began talking . . . to the horse.

"Hey potro . . . potro tranquilo."

Tequito said it over and over, "Hey colt, easy colt." The voice wasn't begging the horse to relax, but it was kind. It was a directive, in the same tone Tequito had used when he said "Mira me" to Wilder. A command, delivered with composure and confidence.

Then his eyes lost the brief kindness that Wilder had seen momentarily, and they were back to their usual look. It wasn't mean, just indifferent. He kept them fixed squarely on the colt's eyes, and they stared each other down for long seconds, separated by 25 feet of rawhide. Wilder did as he was told, staying still and watching.

Finally the colt's eyes fell, and he dropped his head; immediately Tequito fed him enough slack so that the rope touched the ground in between them. Bluebonnet lowered his head to inches above the ground and began licking his lips and acting like he was grazing, but he never took a mouthful. He moved his head back and forth showing his teeth and pink gums and tongue. Wilder had never noticed this kind of behavior from a horse before.

It seemed to be a cue Tequito was waiting for. He moved up the reata with slow but deliberate steps now, eyes off the horse and on the ground in front of him. He took in reata coils one at a time in unbroken motion, all the time repeating "Potro tranquilo."

Never breaking his gait, he walked right up to Bluebonnet's head, the loop still resting loosely on the horse's neck, and stood in front of him. Bluebonnet raised his head slowly, making loud and exaggerated breathing noises through his flaring nostrils. In and out he breathed nervous. He stamped one foot hard against the ground.

Tequito stood absolutely still in front of him, eyes now on the colt's eyes. Bluebonnet kept up the heavy breathing, but starting at Tequito's boot, gently touched it with his nose and sniffed and nibbled a little with his top lip, leaving slobber on the dusty leather. He used his lip like a finger and worked up Tequito's pant leg and scorpion belt buckle and stomach and finally to his chest, snorting and nibbling. The exploration left a streak of brown and green horse saliva on Tequito, which he didn't seem to mind.

Then Tequito squatted down. He took his hat off and held it in one hand against his chest, the reata coils in the other. When his head was about chest high on the colt he put his face out a little and began making exaggerated breathing noises just like the colt. He breathed in and out, as deeply as he could. Bluebonnet brought his flaring nostrils about an inch from Tequito's mouth, and man and horse breathed and snorted back and forth to each other. Bluebonnet arched his neck a few times the way a stud horse might, but he never laid his ears back. In between breaths Tequito whispered, "Potro tranquilo."

After a long minute of this, Tequito stood up and walked away without ever touching the colt. He returned to where Wilder was, 30 feet away with his back to the horse. Then he repeated the whole process two more times. Wilder just watched, in awe.

By the end of the third session, Tequito had tied a new honda, a small fixed loop, on the free end of his reata. The primary loop was still around Bluebonnet's neck. With this honda he built a small loop of rope and then reached out and touched the colt, for the first time, on the right front hock. Tequito tugged at the hock, wanting the horse to release it to him. The colt gave in after ten seconds of hand pressure and lifted his leg slightly. Very quickly Tequito slipped the loop over the foot. The loop was cinched tight around the hock now and the horse placed it back on the ground. Bluebonnet appeared almost to be in a stupor.

Tequito then removed the large loop from Bluebonnet's neck. He walked about ten feet from the front of the colt and put a bit of pressure on the loop that was now on the colt's hock. The colt looked down and snorted and sniffed the rope, now strangely in a new place. He pulled back and reared a bit, to which Tequito responded with slack, but then he pulled the rope taut again. His eyes were locked on the colt.

Tequito pulled, and the foot came forward, dragging on the ground. It wasn't a step, but the colt was giving in to the pressure. "Potro bien. Potro bien," the vaquero encouraged—and commanded.

Tequito pulled again, prompting the colt to take a step, this time necessitating a shift in all four feet to move his body forward in the direction of the two humans. It was going to be the first movement in the young horse's life that the colt would willingly make towards people. Tequito was asking, not forcing.

Bluebonnet took the step, about ten inches towards the pair.

"Good colt, good colt," Wilder heard again, in Spanish.

Tequito kept this up and slowly but consistently began to move around the grass trap leading the colt by the foot. Eyes always locked on the colt, he never demanded too much. When the colt seemed relaxed, he asked for more steps; when the colt looked confused, he gave some slack. But always the intensity of the rope and the commanding gaze of Tequito held the colt's attention. The vaquero had complete control.

Tequito did this work for about an hour, switching the loop back and forth on both front legs. He rubbed the reata coils all over the horse, gently at first, then slopping them on his head and neck and across his withers. He brushed his hand up and down the colt's face and muzzle and neck always talking in a smooth even tone, "Potro bien, potro bien . . ."

Tequito picked up the halter, which Wilder had dropped in the pen. He held the halter in front of the colt and let him sniff this new object that felt and smelled like men—one that had recently been in the hands of a human and used as a whip. But the colt trusted Tequito by this time, and soon he fitted it around the colt's head and tied the rope halter snug against his jowl. Tequito led the horse with both leads now, the roped front foot and with some pressure now on the halter. Bluebonnet accepted this, and followed the man around the pen, turning left and right and stopping and backing up, if clumsily.

The blood from the two scrapes which had occurred during the attempted gate escape had dried. Minor cuts that the horse no longer felt.

Wilder stood still in amazement the whole time. He shifted his feet occasionally when he felt one of them falling asleep. He had never seen anything like this. He had never heard of anything like this. He watched, and he learned.

CHAPTER NINE

Halters and Leads

Tequito led the colt to the thickest cedar post on the corral fence. He checked it by kicking the dirt around its base and trying to wiggle it with both hands. Assured it was tightly secured by prairie clay against a green colt, he slipped the reata off the colt's foot and tied the halter lead to the grayed post. He tied the horse short and high, leaving only about a foot of lead rope between halter and post. He rubbed the horse some more, speaking all along, and then retreated across the pen, climbed the fence, and went to his pickup. He grabbed a big canvas bag and reseated himself under the cottonwood tree where he had begun the day.

Again, Wilder wasn't sure what to do. But he knew that he had to fix the gate that his anger and inexperience had caused Bluebonnet to destroy. It was a worn wood gate and while it had held for many years, under the stress of a frightened horse it had sort of exploded. Papa was going to be upset, he figured.

Wilder felt somewhat relieved to let Bluebonnet be. He threw the gate pieces over the fence where he could drag them to the barn. He walked over to Tequito, figuring he should check in to see if he should be doing anything with the colt. He made eye contact from inside the pen with the seated Tequito, who was working big knots of rawhide string, braiding them in his lap. Tequito looked up and knew from Wilder's expression he was about to ask what he should do.

"Potro bien," he said to the boy. Wilder got the message and said, "Gracias." He walked past Bluebonnet on the way to the barn. The colt looked at him and began stomping his right foot on the ground. He pulled back on the halter, testing the confinement he felt for the first time in his life.

Wilder spent the next four hours in the machine shed, a small lean-to on the larger barn. He laid out the gate and salvaged all the hardware, taking measurements first and marking them on the wall with cutting torch chalk. He was a pretty good carpenter for age 12, having built things with his dad since he could remember.

Papa came through once around 11:00. He

didn't say anything, although Wilder caught him from the corner of his eye observing what he was doing. The old man grabbed a can of WD-40 and walked out again without saying anything.

Wilder went to the house after 1:00, when the gate was rebuilt and ready to hang. He would need another set of hands to hang it. From the dishes in the sink he could tell Papa and Tequito had eaten together. Papa was asleep in his chair now, and Wilder made a quick lunch of Marisol's enchiladas.

When Wilder returned to the pens, he saw that Tequito had taken a nap too, propped up on his canvas bag under the tree. Bluebonnet had given up foot-stomping and stood in the hot sun on three legs. Tequito raised up when he saw him and met him at the pens. Tequito pointed to the barn and said "Listo?" Wilder didn't know what "listo" meant but he assumed it meant Tequito was offering to help. So he said "si," and the two walked to the barn together in silence.

After they had hung the gate and secured the colt's pen, Tequito nodded at Wilder and said once more, "Mira me."

He untied Bluebonnet, all the while stroking and talking to him, and led him to the water tank. Wilder noticed a three-foot-wide hole in

the ground where Bluebonnet's hoof had engraved his impatience into the sod. Bluebonnet drank, and Tequito slipped off the halter
without the colt knowing. He kept his arm
around the colt and grabbed a handful of mane
in the middle of his neck. After allowing for a
long drink Tequito tugged with his arm hold
and a little pressure on the mane and took a
few steps away from the tank with the colt.
The colt followed, and then Tequito let go. He
turned his back to the colt and walked away.
Bluebonnet followed without the halter. Again,
Wilder was speechless.

Tequito turned around and re-caught the colt
with his arm and mane. He took steps again
and the colt led without resistance. Again he
let go and again Bluebonnet followed. After repeating this sequence several more times, Tequito gently pushed the horse's head sideways
and slipped the other way, letting the colt
know he was free now. Finally Bluebonnet understood and wandered back to the water tank.

Tequito looked to see if Wilder had been
watching. He believed the boy had seen everything. The vaquero didn't smile with any par-
ticular pride, but he began to think that Wilder
had the sensitive intelligence of a horseman. A
job was a job to him, but for the first time in
a while, he felt as though he was accomplish-

ing something greater than just another saddle horse.

Tequito liked America, and he liked Texas, and he had longed most of his life to join his big brother on a ranch in Texas and make a name for himself training horses there. Americans paid a lot more than Mexicans. But he had a secret, now 30 years old, that still directed his life.

Artemio first came to Texas on a green card when he was 18 and Tequito was still a boy in Jalisco, earning his nickname as the Little Tick. Artemio did well with hard work and learning English and by the time he was 30 years old he was settled in the Texas panhandle with a wife and two kids and U.S. citizenship. Tequito visited often, but Artemio never offered to let his brother live with him.

Tequito was wild. The bad kind of wild.

On a return trip to Mexico, when he was 20, he had stabbed a white college student outside a bar in Las Cruces. It was a typical young man's fight, fueled by loose words and subtle differences in skin tone . . . The night was a blur to him now, but he had made it across the border to Juarez and eventually back to Jalisco and no one ever seemed to know or suspect anything.

It had happened quick, as that kind of violence tends to do, but it sat like a rock in his stomach for 30 years. Tequito had his own cuts from the fight and heard that the student had lived, and so life went on. What he did remember is that while it wasn't premeditated, he had felt the rise of anger and violence in his heart, and he had given in to it. For a few seconds he felt nothing, only power. The memory of those moments scared him for the rest of his life. And he never entered a bar again.

Shortly after the fight Tequito lost his right thumb. He was gathering wild strays in heavy mesquite brush on a big ranch in Jalisco. Pastures covered thousands of acres, and only young vaqueros would take the job since it was dangerous and paid little. Tequito liked it. The cattle were feral as deer and sulled in the mesquite and cactus. A horse was rarely able to work all day, and then was prone to going lame and needed rest.

Tequito wasn't scared of anything, and he took more chances than he should have, which only built his reputation as a good *brassero* or "hand" with livestock. But the difference in a hero and hubris is sometimes thin, and that line was crossed one day when a young bull that Tequito roped far from the ranch corrals broke for a deep arroyo at feeling the reata tighten on its muscle-layered neck. Tequito had to loosen his dally and follow the bull for a bit to get a closer tie before it got into the deep crevice in the land.

The bull made a last charge for the arroyo, and Tequito took a quick dally on his horn, cocky with his ability to contain the animal. But his thumb hung up on the reata and was wrapped into the dally. It was stuck between the rapidly tightening rope and the enraged 1,500-pound bull lurching for the brush. The rope tensed straight like a shot, and his thumb bone broke with a pop, and the skin was pinched off by the coils.

Tequito's hand shot up and he dropped the coils and reins from the other. The bull had control of the saddle and the horse now, and its pull jerked everything to the ground. Horse and rider were dragged through ten feet of prickly pear cactus. The dallies on the saddle horn came loose, finally freeing man and horse. The bull disappeared trailing 55 feet of hand-braided reata, several feet now marked in red.

Tequito was in bad shape, but instead of feeling anger or panic, he felt calm. He knew his luck had worn thin in many things and lying there bleeding with a prickly pear palm embedded in his ear and cheek . . . he thought back to Las Cruces. His body went cold and he never said a word as he wrapped a tourniquet around his thumb and proceeded to pull three inch cactus spines from his horse, and then from his own body.

As he walked back to the ranch house in the dark hours and miles later, holding his bloody hand, still covered in broken-off cactus spines, and trailed by a loose, limping horse, Tequito imagined that God was paying him back. He never searched for the thumb. He figured a coyote, or maybe a pack rat, would eat it.

After that day he felt somewhat cleansed of his sins. He wasn't able to ride or make money for months, but he felt relieved as the pain and the recovery from the accident worked through him. He started praying to his saint, and going to the cathedral in town.

But whether real or imaginary, Tequito feared the border for the rest of his life. He knew better than to ever register for a green card or visa. He never knew if he was hunted or if his face was posted on a board somewhere. So he stayed in Mexico, never married, and lost himself in horses.

Horses, colts especially, took an almost spiritual focus that he craved. It took a willingness to completely dominate a horse mentally. The concentration on a hundred subtleties and the planned yet immediate reaction to each one drove him. He thought like a horse almost completely, becoming simply a dominant mare or stud when he was with them. As a part of the herd, he doled out punishment and grace as was necessary to shape a horse's will to his own. He replaced all his wildness and arrogance with patience and understanding, but with the same fervor.

And now he was in the U.S. for the first time since, at Artemio's repeated request. Thirty-two years later, not even his big brother knew his secret.

Tequito spent the evening with the rest of Papa's remuda, taking them one by one through their paces and working up a lather. He pushed all their buttons, finding holes in their obedience or training, and patching them up with smooth but firm adjustments. He still loved doing it, but he also liked that Wilder was sitting on the fence watching him.

Before he drove back to Artemio's for the night, he attempted some communication with Wilder. He looked at him and said, "Con caballos . . . fuerte aqui," and he pointed to his head. "Nada fuerte aqui," and he pointed to his bicep. He hoped the boy understood where strength with horses came from, among other things.

June 17
    I don't know where to start.
    I crashed Bluebonnet through the gate. Papa hired a Mexican vaquero to help, Tequito, and he roped Bluebonnet as he was escaping. He did it with a reata (coolest rope ever). His loop was a hoolihan, which I hadn't seen before either. I threw about 100 of them tonight. I learned don't rope a horse if you don't know what you are doing.
    Tequito showed me how to break a horse to lead. We got the halter on and I ended up leading Bluebonnet all over the place. I talk to him and pet him all over. Tequito said he is muy intelligente.
    I made a lot of mistakes to start with, but tonight I feel completely different about everything with horses.
    Papa was right. I didn't know what I knew.

ᘺᏻ

CHAPTER TEN
First Ride

The next day followed much the same pattern. Wilder worked the young horse, except he was patient and gentle now, and Tequito filled in the gaps. Awkwardly at first, and then becoming more natural, the boy and man began an almost wordless conversation about horses. With eye contact or lack of it, tone of voice in short words and phrases, and subtle hand gestures, they moved through Bluebonnet's training. When he needed a mental rest, they worked the other horses in the remuda.

Papa had brought the rest of the horses into the pens on the other side of the barn. It was best to keep the others away from the colt to prevent distraction. Sometimes a colt was worked with an older broke horse if it needed another horse's presence to keep calm. Bluebonnet was doing fine on his own, which was better.

Tequito checked in with Papa about the proper bits he should use on the other horses, but he rode his own saddle. That was another thing Wilder had never seen or even heard of, a Mexican saddle.

It looked markedly different from all of Papa's. The first thing Wilder noticed was the horn, which was four times as big as a regular saddle horn. It was round and white, covered in a dried, tight rawhide, and the top tilted up towards the horse's head like a mountain peak. There was no leather on the tree or roping rubber under the horn. It looked like a dinner plate—a dinner plate with burnished silver rope engraved and embedded around the top of the horn.

The saddle was single-rigged, one-cinch. It had rawhide lace-work all over the sparse leather portions and no leather tooling designs. A pair of saddle bags hung off the back which were incorporated into the design of the saddle skirt. Tequito's bridle, breast collar, and spur straps matched it perfectly in design and wear.

Tequito wore brass spurs with boot heel shapes for the boot shanks and a screaming eagle engraved on the spur shank, which spun a thin but large wheel of 10 spikes. Tequito didn't have to use them much, but when he did, he got the horse's attention.

On the outside of the shanks was a silver inlaid eight-legged tick.

The vaquero's gear was the most exotic collection Wilder's small-town eyes had ever seen.

He liked them. It made him wonder what
else he didn't know about the world.

Tequito backed off Bluebonnet completely
on day two, staying out of the pen, wanting
the horse to bond only with Wilder to learn
the boy's smell and movements. Wilder would
watch Tequito on another horse, and then rep-
licate everything he saw on Bluebonnet. Tequito touched and patted and smoothed the
coat of a five-year-old mare that was broke
but seldom ridden, and then he slipped quietly
onto the horse's bare back and reined her with
the halter.

Wilder meant to try the same with Bluebonnet by the end of day two. He had tested the
colt's tolerance for his weight all day by gently
hanging on his neck and then by belly flopping
on his back from both sides. When Bluebonnet
seemed to get uncomfortable, he would slide
back to the ground. Tequito could tell Wilder
was going to try for a first ride, bareback, and
moved close to the pen, but he didn't climb in.

Wilder made his belly flop move and he
held the lead, now looped around the colt's
neck and tied back to the halter to make a set
of reins. Balanced, he began to swing his leg
over. The boy's belly fluttered—he knew this

was the point of no return. Without pausing he completed the action. He now had a leg on either side of the horse.

He was riding Bluebonnet.

He wiggled slightly and found his middle and then laid his torso down along the colt's neck. He whispered to him "potro bien" just like Tequito.

Bluebonnet bent his head around sideways and sniffed and nibbled at the boy's boots. On one side and then the other, as if confirming with his eyes . . . that there was person on his back. The colt took a step, then a couple more, then stopped. Tequito and Wilder both watched the colt's ears. They flirted with pinning back a few times, but always came back to a center-and-forward position as Wilder patted and spoke to the nervous horse.

Wilder sat up straight, fully astride his colt. He couldn't believe it. He thought the first ride would be a big showdown between man and beast to see who was toughest. There would be a winner and a loser, and he had felt the loser would eventually be the horse, no matter what. But now he was there, sort of, and it had seemed kind of easy. Bluebonnet had come his way, and Wilder had come the horse's way a lot, he admitted to himself. It had only been about 24 hours since the rodeo of the day before. Everything he thought about horse breaking had been turned upside down.

He looked over at Tequito, and they smiled at each other. Wilder asked with his eyes what to do next. Tequito made a little clicking sound with his lips and shook his hand as if he was giving a loose rein to a horse. Wilder was surprised, but nodded. He loosened up his seat a bit and shook the reins. Tequito wanted to see the horse move now, under the weight of a rider.

Bluebonnet was content to stay put. The colt wasn't upset about the boy being on top of him, but he wasn't ready to experiment with walking. Wilder gave him a little kick with his boot heels, which wore no spurs. Tequito had motioned earlier for him to take them off for now. The heels were just a gentle nudge, but it was consistent pressure in the ribs that was new and uncomfortable. Bluebonnet hunched his middle up in reaction, and his ears went back.

Wilder looked at Tequito. Tequito made a hard face and pointed to his eyes and then pointed at the horse as if to say, "Pay attention to him, not to me." Wilder focused on the colt's ears and gripped with his thighs. He had been taught to ride bareback by Papa when he was little and so was not unaccustomed to it now. However, riding a skinny colt with no leather handles was different. He felt like he was strad-dling a fence rail five feet off the ground.

"Potro bien," he assured the horse out loud. He said it with a gentle but commanding voice, as he had heard Tequito do. He waited for the ears to relax and point forward, and he gave the horse another nudge with his seat and heels.

Bluebonnet bunched up quickly and took a clumsy leap forward. All four feet left the ground. He wasn't trying to throw Wilder off, he just didn't know what to do with the weight and the heel pressure. Wilder was as ready as he could have been. He grabbed two handholds of black mane and held on. When Bluebonnet hit the ground, he went into a trot and started circling the pen.

Wilder slipped off to the left side but wouldn't give up. He dug his right heel and leg into the horse and gripped and pulled with his hamstrings. Bluebonnet was bouncing pretty good in an aimless trot, but Wilder held on. He inched back up and regained his center. Mounted in the middle again, he gave Bluebon-net his head on a loose rein.

He didn't try to rein the horse left or right; he just let him travel. When he stopped, Wilder let him rest. After a few seconds and neck pats, he nudged him back into gear. Bluebonnet never jumped or bucked or laid his ears back

again. He just moved around the pen, sometimes walking, sometimes trotting, as if having
a human on his back was natural. Wilder was
using every muscle in his body like a horseman does, tense and ready from head to heels.
He quickly tired and after five minutes was
content to let Bluebonnet stand. He sat there
catching his breath and turned back to Tequito.
The vaquero nodded and said, "Bien," making a
flat hand movement.

Wilder slipped off and led Bluebonnet over to
the vaquero. Bluebonnet had a sweat-darkened
coat from the ride, and his nostrils heaved as
both the horse's mind and body calmed down
from the event. Tequito and Wilder smiled
at each other in approval. The first ride was
over. Tequito said, "Muy intelligente," pointing
toward Bluebonnet.

They left Bluebonnet in the square pen haltered and tied on the cedar post. Standing
tied was an important skill to learn as well,
and it was best taught by a good halter and a
cedar post.

In the evening after supper, Tequito pulled a
grass rope, a *soga*, out of his pickup. He showed
off a bit turning some amazing loops in the
air and jumping through them. The rope art-
istry was part of the Jalisco rodeo tradition
called the *Charreria*. Wilder grabbed his rope

and started trying the twirls and loops. Papa enjoyed the show but knew he would never attempt that type of roping. That was the difference between cowboys and vaqueros owing in part to the relative ages of the traditions; cowboys just wanted to get it done, vaqueros wanted it to look beautiful.

Tequito drove off while it was still light out. Papa sat on the front porch reading. Wilder went out to Bluebonnet and went through the paces of leading and haltering and handling and talking. Feeling a little brave perhaps, he let Bluebonnet out into the grass trap which covered more than a hundred acres. It hadn't been grazed this year and was covered with buffalo and grama grass and big and little bluestem. Bluebonnet greedily grazed the tender sod grasses. Dotted all through the pasture were wildflowers; Indian blankets with their red and yellow petals, white lazy daisies, purple rounded colonies of prairie winecup, and orangish-yellow Mexican hats. The previous fall had been wet and so despite the current drought, the hardiest wildflowers had germinated and now bloomed in low places that had caught the most moisture.

Wilder checked for ants and then lay down and watched the cotton from the cottonwood trees float as the country quietly went to sleep.

He heard Bluebonnet's slurpy wet grazing. The horse would gather blades of grass, sorting weeds out with his top lip, then bite and rip the mouthful.

He lay there until past sundown. Walking back to the house he realized that the colt was following him. He had no halter or lead, but Bluebonnet had his head down, watching Wilder and following him about ten feet behind. Feeling happy and a bit mischievous Wilder stopped abruptly, jumped up, and turned a quick 180 degrees in the air. He threw his hands up and whooped right in Bluebonnet's unsuspecting face.

The colt jumped up and spun crazily, breaking wind in the process which made Wilder holler with laughter. Bluebonnet pranced away from him with his tail up, looking back over his shoulder. Wilder gave chase.

He stopped after 50 feet and then turned and ran back the way he had been walking toward the house. Bluebonnet stopped his prancing too, and ran back toward Wilder to catch up. Wilder couldn't believe it. When Bluebonnet seemed relaxed and walking behind him again, he turned and jumped again. The colt snorted and ran off.

This time Wilder ran as fast as he could for a sandhill plum thicket on the edge of the grass trap. He huddled behind the forest of five-foot-tall shrubs and waited. Slowly Bluebonnet began stalking the boy. The horse soon found him and blew hot air and horse boogers all over his downed neck as he held his hiding position. Wilder played dead, enjoying the sweat and breath of Bluebonnet, and decided that horses had the best smell of any animal. Finally he shot up and chased Bluebonnet back across the pen.

Wilder hid behind every soapberry tree, yucca, and sandhill plum for the next hour, and each time Bluebonnet found him. They played a breathless cat and mouse game until it was pitch dark. Wilder laughed, and the young horse kicked and bucked and snorted until they both stood and stared at each other under nothing but stars. Wilder didn't know a horse would do that.

Wilder wrote two entries in his journal that night. One was a letter to Sunny, his friend, who was a girl.

June 18
  I rode Bluebonnet today. Bareback. I didn't plan to, it just happened. He let me.
  It might have been the best day of my life. I should probably say more about it but I don't think I can.

Sunny,

  I am in Texas at Papa's ranch. He gave me a colt to break that is my own horse. I am figuring it out with a vaquero cowboy. His name is Bluebonnet. The horse, not the vaquero. I played hide and go seek with my horse tonight in the grass trap. You would have liked it.

  I have been reading Papa's books down here and a bunch are all about the Comanches. Their real name for themselves is the Numina. It means 'The People'. They come up with awesome names for themselves that I never knew about. Well, the reason I am writing is that I came up with a name for you tonight. I wasn't trying to come up with a name for you but I just did.

  I think your Numina name should be Wildflowers-in-her-Hair. That's pretty much it.

                                    Wilder

CHAPTER ELEVEN

Purpose

"Papa, can I drive to the mailbox and mail a letter?"

They had just eaten breakfast, and Wilder asked his question very casually as if he always drove the pickup by himself. Papa had let him drive before, and he had been driving tractors and four-wheelers since he was big enough to steer in his Dad's lap. But still, this was a bluff that Wilder hoped to shoot right past the old man.

"Come right back," Papa replied with a serious look.

Wilder forced himself to walk slowly off the porch and over to the pickup. He was hoping he would pass Tequito on his way in to the ranch for the day's horse work, or any other cowboy or rancher for that matter. They could stop their pickups and talk in the middle of the road as if Wilder was a grownup.

He deposited his letter, and then crept back down the road in the big diesel. He didn't meet anyone coming or going. After parking the truck, Wilder asked Papa if he had heard from Tequito. He had been there at dawn the last two mornings.

"No, I haven't heard from him. He didn't promise anything more than a day or two."

"Should I just keep working with Bluebonnet then?"

"Sure. It looks like you are doing fine."

Papa had been watching, even though he had been sneaky about it. He was watching for safety, but also out of pride, which he couldn't express to Wilder. Praise had always embarrassed Papa, and he just assumed everybody else felt the same way. He also didn't really know the man Tequito, or how he would act with a kid. Papa was pleased with both of them.

Wilder walked out to the corrals. Bluebonnet had been left in the grass trap the night before. Wilder grabbed the halter and lead and the excitement and confidence he had developed over the past two days began to dissipate like the morning's cool air. He swallowed the fear and hopped the fence and knew he had to fake courage until it came naturally. He wondered when he would just simply always be brave.

Bluebonnet nickered to him, and he caught the colt easily. The horse was no longer just a wild animal. He wasn't broke yet either, but he knew enough to cross over that invisible line that separated coltish ignorance from the simultaneously painful and wonderful stage of understanding his purpose.

Wilder spent the next three days putting Bluebonnet through all the paces he could think of. He brushed and led him, and rode him bareback in the small pen. He brought his saddle and blankets into the pen and gave the horse several hours to sniff and get used to them. He saddled Bluebonnet for the first time and lounged him on a long lead around the pen. He showed the horse his spurs and where they would hang when he rode.

Wilder then began to ride the colt with a saddle. He used a hackamore bridle, which was a large rawhide noseband connected to two cotton leads. Wilder stayed in the corral and let the horse walk around, slowly getting used to having his face pulled one way or the other. The reining came slowest of all, but Wilder was patient. He was learning right along with the colt. Wilder rode until the insides of his knees were rubbed raw and took on a blue fuzz texture from the denim of his jeans wearing off and sticking to the sores.

Bluebonnet, Papa said, like his mother Fancy years before, took everything in stride, seeming to enjoy the process of learning. He never bucked. He never acted like he had a mean streak about anything.

Wilder followed Tequito's rules in all that he did; he went slow, he applied pressure and released pressure, and he used his brain, not his muscles. The anger he had fallen into the first day seemed foreign now, like something childish from kindergarten that he had long since graduated from.

In the evenings, Wilder would take his dinner out to the pens and eat with Bluebonnet. He found that the horse liked tortillas, and so the supply of Marisol's tortillas quickly disappeared. Papa noticed. Wilder figured they weren't sugary so it wasn't a treat. He turned on the radio in the barn, and he thought Bluebonnet took a liking to George Strait. Wilder didn't have any real evidence of this but he liked the idea. Every night they played hide and go seek until dark.

Wilder hadn't had a bath all week which he didn't notice until he witnessed Coffee roll in a fresh cow pie. The dumb dog had rolled and coated herself green from ear to tail and Wilder knew he wasn't going to sleep with a dog in that condition. In the process of dowsing her in the stock tank he got considerably wet himself. Blue heelers hate being in water, unlike his dog back home, Huck, a yellow lab. So he decided to strip down and bathe as well. He found a few ticks between the dog's shoulders in the process, pinched them off and chunked them.

Bluebonnet joined in and thrashed the water with his nose. He kept it up, and Wilder was sure he was no longer drinking. He was playing with them. The horse even got his front feet into the tank and began stomping the water, sending wave after wave into the boy and dog's face. Wilder laughed over and over again as Papa watched from the porch. The old man almost wished he was with them, knowing that kind of fun was only in his past. Wilder was a good grandson, and he felt a little pride that the week had gone better than he had expected.

Wilder dried in his white underwear, lying out on the still-warm front walk flagstones like a snake. That night he and Papa watched *Captain Blood* with Errol Flynn. Wilder had never seen it before and he thought it was about the best movie ever. He hollered at the TV, "He is in for a surprise!" both times the bad guy Bishop was about to get duped by Captain Blood. When Blood said "brotherhood of buccaneers," Wilder thought pirating would be a good second job to cowboying.

They ate boiled ham hocks and lambs quarters, a wild green that Wilder had found in the corrals. Papa was skeptical at first, but when Wilder showed him the plant in his own wildflower book he agreed and enjoyed them. Wilder found an old carton of Blue Bell ice cream in the big freezer in the garage. It was mint chocolate chip which Wilder hated but he and Papa ate it anyway. Wilder tried not to think about how old the green ice cream was.

On Saturday, Tequito showed up again. Wilder and Papa were surprised and happy to see him sitting in his pickup drinking coffee from a thermos cup when they came out of the house at 7 am. The three of them assembled under the cottonwoods and stared at Bluebonnet in the corral. Tequito could tell that Wilder had been saddling and riding him by the large rectangular sweat stains made by the saddle blankets.

"Nada problemas con Azul?" Tequito asked. He had started calling the horse "Blue" in Spanish. Papa waited for Wilder to answer. It was a rare privilege for a boy to get asked a real question among men. Tequito was showing him respect.

"Potro bien," Wilder said and smiled. It was the truth, but it also stood as kind of a code phrase between the two of them. Those two words marked the beginning of his horse education—for both Wilder and Bluebonnet.

Papa and Tequito rambled back and forth in their Spanish and English and then made their way to the porch and inside. Coffee and Wilder followed after feeding Bluebonnet his hay and small coffee can of oats. They all sat down at the kitchen table and Papa offered Tequito biscuits and a breakfast burrito. He ate a biscuit and the two men drank coffee as Wilder watched. Wilder was anxious to show Tequito everything he could do on Bluebonnet.

After a casual Spanglish conversation that lasted through two cups of coffee, Papa stood up and said he had to go work on the rodent problem. This meant he was going to mix a batch of poison with oats and sprinkle it in the appropriate spots around the house and barns and specific pastures where there were no livestock. Vermin on a ranch can get out of hand and become a risk several different ways if not treated from time to time. Knowing he might not see Tequito again, Papa went to his room and came back with an envelope containing cash for three days work. He handed it to him and purposefully didn't make eye contact. Neither did Tequito as he quickly tucked the envelope into his brush jacket. Outside they shook hands, and Papa said "Gracias" and "mucho gusto."

Tequito never counted the money.

Wilder soon caught Bluebonnet and tied him to the cedar post. Tequito took up his position underneath the cottonwood tree. Wilder saddled his colt and pulled the cinch tight. He no longer needed to baby the horse. He walked across the pen to show Tequito the rawhide hackamore he had been using, hoping to gain approval. Tequito stood up and handled it, checking the braiding and strength of the rawhide. It was good he thought, not as good as the ones he made himself, but good enough for Texans.

Wilder put it on Bluebonnet and walked him to the middle of the pen, checking that everything was feeling good to the horse. And then without any pause, he grabbed a bit of mane and stepped up with his left leg and swung his right leg over like he was riding a tired old circus pony. He wiggled to get his seat deep and find the middle. His back was straight and firm. He extended his heels down and pointed his toes up and felt the visceral satisfaction of being horseback.

He didn't look to Tequito for approval. Not because he was arrogant, but he knew it was right, now, to move without seeking affirmation. Wilder rode around the pen, asking the horse slowly for all the things they had practiced—reining, stopping, backing, standing, walking, and trotting. The boy moved with confidence and in step physically and mentally with the horse. They were a team working together. Tequito was impressed but not surprised.

They spent the rest of the day working Bluebonnet. They talked often. It was amazing how much they had learned to communicate, and built on the foundation already laid with the colt. Wilder began twirling a rope on the ground and then from the saddle. Tequito threw a heavy downed tree limb into the pen and Wilder started dragging it, dallied to his saddle. He kicked the horse into a lope at the end of the day, which was pretty rough, but Bluebonnet figured out the new gait and Wilder held on.

After dinner, just before dusk, Tequito left. He seemed reluctant. In one sense he was doing what he loved to do, like always, like in Mexico. But he was enjoying this new company and how receptive this boy had been to his teaching. He didn't know when, but he hoped he would be back.

Wilder knew his visit had changed his life. He didn't know how to say that, and didn't know if he should, even if he did have the words. He shook Tequito's hand and said, "Gracias." Tequito slapped him on the back and turned to his truck.

Standing in the front yard, Papa nodded to himself and slapped Wilder on the back too. He turned to walk to the barn, its big front door still open. "Take a real bath tonight," Papa said, "We have church in the morning."

From inside the house the phone rang, and they both figured it was Livy or Hank, Wilder's parents, calling to check in. The pair went inside and didn't come back out until the next morning. That night Wilder wrote a poem.

June 22

Bluebonnet is going great. Tequito told Papa over and over that my horse is muy intelligente. I saddled and rode him most of the day, but not in the big pastures. He spooked at a bunch of quail in the plum thicket and I fell off, but I got right back on.

I gave him a vaccine for tetanus, several viruses, and west nile. I also gave him a mouth paste for worms. Papa said all this was silly but he got it for me at Gebo's anyway.

Mom and Dad said tonight that it was OK to stay another week with Papa. Bluebonnet needs more work and I hope to start taking rides outside of the grass trap this week.

I think I might go to Mexico when I get bigger and cowboy there awhile. My hoolihan throw is getting better.

Bluebonnet black coat
Like a starry sky,
Velvet light in night
Drips in my eye.

Too big to hold,
Too beautiful to miss,
Heaven and a horse,
What am I to this?

CHAPTER TWELVE

'How do we fix it?'

Papa and Wilder never made it to church.
Wilder came bouncing out of the house at 7 am in his basketball shorts to feed his horse. From the porch he looked over to Bluebonnet's pen and didn't see him. He saw that the barn door was open, which was unusual, but not any big deal. There weren't any animals in there, just tools and hay and the tack room.

Wilder had left the gate open to the grass trap like usual and he figured Bluebonnet was grazing in the lush hundred acre pasture. He walked around the side of the pen with his eyes to the grass trap and started whistling. Bluebonnet wouldn't come to him the way a dog would, but it let the horse know Wilder was around. He usually perked up and whinnied.

The grass trap was big and full of brush and several cottonwood and soapberry trees, so it wasn't a surprise that Wilder didn't see the horse right off. But after walking around for a few minutes and checking all their hiding spots, he began to get nervous. Bluebonnet wasn't in the trap.

Then he saw it.

The gate from the grass trap to the barnyard was open. Wilder wasn't sure, but perhaps he had left it open yesterday as he took all the day's horse gear back to the tack room in the barn. His heart beat fast, nervous about his mistake, and he jogged back to the house to tell Papa. Every acre of the ranch was fenced, so Bluebonnet couldn't be out on the road, but he was somewhere running loose.

Papa told him that was fine and that they would find him. The old man finished his cup of coffee and left it on the table for Coffee the dog to finish—which she did, hopping up on the kitchen table and lapping down the black liquid.

Papa and Wilder walked straight toward the big concrete stock tank in the middle of the corral. When they got close, Papa saw it before Wilder did. He was a foot taller and so could see over the tank before the boy could.

A blue roan colt lay on the ground on the other side of the tank. It was Bluebonnet and the old man knew the horse was dead.

Papa stopped abruptly and put a hand out to stop the boy. Another few feet and he would be at the tank's edge and be able to see over the top.

Wilder looked up at his Papa, wide-eyed, immediately nervous at the action.

"What is it Papa?" Wilder whispered, going into his hunting voice.

The old man was stunned. He had seen plenty of dead animals before but never as unexpected as this. He took a second to compose himself. His voice cracked when he spoke. It wasn't in a whisper. "Wilder, something happened to your horse." He didn't know what else to do, so he nodded with his head and pointed to the tank with his eyes.

Wilder ran forward and soon saw the strange blue-black mass of hair in the corral. He climbed the wood rail fence in seconds and slid down next to the horse's head without hesitation. He petted the colt's cheek softly, not believing what he was seeing. But the boy knew immediately that there was no life, no beating pulse, no warm friendly partner under his hand. His softest spot just under the nose and over the top lip that had searched Wilder's hand last night for a tortilla no longer responded to his touch. The horse lay still, his right eye facing up, still wet under long black lashes.

Wilder started panicking and his head

swam. He stood up and looked for Papa who was now coming up behind him having walked around the side and through the gate. He felt like screaming, but he restrained himself. He looked at Papa.

"Papa, what can we do? We have to get him up!"

Papa leaned down on both knees and started going over the colt with his hands. He took his hat off and laid his ear down flush on the horse's chest, just back from the front shoulder. There was no sound. Papa felt the nostrils and opened the mouth. He touched the big black eye, softly, and nothing happened. No blink, no movement. The old man said "God," quietly, exhaling.

"Wilder," he breathed in and out, "he is dead."

"Papa, how can he be dead? I was just here last night. I fed him and he was fine and we played and there wasn't anything wrong." Wilder's chest heaved in and out and his head filled with a pressure that felt like a balloon that wouldn't pop. Tears were welling up but did not come yet.

"I don't know, son. I don't know what happened. I don't see anything wrong with the horse."

"When I came out to the trap this morning the gate to the barnyard was open. But he didn't leave, he is right here, right where he is supposed to be."

Papa looked up when he heard that. His stomach went queasy, and he knew then what had happened. He left the boy who was petting and saying "Potro bien" to the colt. He walked over to the grass trap gate and looked at the ground. The colt had been through the gate and he didn't have to track it to know where it had been.

Papa walked straight to the barn and went inside through the massive wood sliding door. Next to the workbench in the back, obscured by years of junk and a broken spray rig and a small stack of alfalfa dotted with raccoon droppings, he saw the tell-tale answer. It was the bag of oats he had mixed the rodent poison in. The 50-pound bag was on the floor, the brown paper ripped down the side. He walked over and picked up the feed sack. It read "Whole Oats" and had a picture of a horse on the front, in profile. No oats were left.

He kept the poison locked in an old cabinet in the machine shed. He wasn't careless with it. He knew the strychnine was bad stuff, but he had used it for years, just like his dad and granddad before him. He had never had any problems.

The old man cursed himself. There hadn't been half a coffee can worth of poisoned oats still in the bag when he put it there yesterday. He couldn't believe the horse had actually found them. Thousands of acres to roam and eat grass on, and the colt had found this small batch of poison. Stupid colts. And on the day Wilder happened to leave the gate open. Same day. And he had forgotten to close the barn door.

But he knew it was his fault, and he was heartbroken. Every sadness of his life flooded back to him as he held the bag in the cavernous barn all alone. His head and shoulders sagged, and he wept. Tears streaked down his wrinkled face and zig-zagged on gray whiskers that hadn't been shaved yet this morning. He felt the war from years ago. He felt the passing of his wife Marian, seven years ago. He felt the panic of the day he took the call from Livy, his daughter, saying she had cancer. He felt small and stupid and helpless. He cursed himself again.

He threw the bag down and wiped his eyes and walked out of the barn to tell Wilder.

Wilder was lying on the horse's chest, listening for a heartbeat that would not come. He stroked the horse's face repeatedly up and down, up and down, in a repetition that warmed that small piece of cheek and made it feel alive.

Papa sat down slowly and leaned back against the water tank. He fumbled with Bluebonnet's mane from the other side. He patted the dead horse's neck from habit.

"Wilder, I am sorry. This is my fault." Papa was stoic as he said it, his tears wiped dry but he was still red-faced.

"Bluebonnet got out and got into the poison oats I mixed yesterday. He ate a bunch, and they killed him quick. I am sure of it."

Wilder's face shot up from the horse. He looked at Papa a few feet away, and his mind couldn't seem to understand the words.

"He . . . he ate poison?" The boy was dumbstruck. He stopped petting the horse. He hoped maybe this new information somehow meant they could save him. "How did he eat poison?"

"He found it in the barn. I left it out. It was my fault."

"How do we fix it?" Wilder knew about death and knew this didn't make any sense, but it was all he could say. His mind raced over and over again about what he could do. Wilder loved action, he loved being required to do something heroic, whether real or imaginary. He was ready to do anything.

"Son, there is nothing we can do. He is

dead." Papa said this with a tenderness he had never used with Wilder. He always spoke to him like a man, but this he said as if to a small child. "You see that, don't you?"

"How did he get out?" Wilder asked, realizing when he said it that the gate was open. He had left it open. He knew that.

"I left the gate open, Papa. I think I did anyway. He couldn't have opened it himself."

"Well, whatever happened with the gate . . . it doesn't matter."

With those words the tears broke open inside the boy, and he began to weep, waves of quiet sobs that he buried in the soft sweet smell of his horse. Papa sat for a second, then got up and went into the house.

Wilder never left the pen except to get a brush and curry comb. He stroked and petted his horse all over, lost in the wilderness of his grief. He felt the massive body go slowly from warm and loose, to cold and stiff. All day he sat with his horse as the cottonwoods rustled above him and the sun crossed over the corral stretching shadows long one way, and then the other.

ᘺ

CHAPTER THIRTEEN

'To own a horse'

Papa let his grandson be. He called Livy after lunch and told her they had missed church and then told her the rest of the story. She cried over the phone for her father and for her son, and knew the sorrow that was rolling over her happy childhood home, the Tree Water ranch. "I love you, Dad," she said several times. Papa knew that was true, but he felt foolish, a foolish old man who had lived too long.

After that he took some food to Wilder with a frozen gallon milk jug of water that he always kept in the garage deep freeze. He knew it would thaw and keep cold throughout the day. Wilder didn't touch the food or water.

Around six o'clock Papa felt he should break the boy's fast, and going to the evening church service seemed like a good excuse. He went out and told Wilder they were leaving for church in 30 minutes and he needed to get ready. Wilder obeyed, listless but polite, and went to his room and changed out of the basketball

Green   Colt

shorts and t-shirt he had been in all day. He ate a banana and glass of milk in the truck on the way to Verbena. Neither of them spoke. Neither was upset at the other, and they weren't pouting, there just weren't any words. Their grief was like the ranch after the sun went down, everything was black.

Evening service was simple and small, only 15 or so people. Wilder felt ashamed for hoping Tequito and Artemio would not be there. He couldn't bear to face them. They didn't show—and yet he was sad when they didn't walk in after the opening prayer.

Clarence greeted them with an eye wink when Papa and Wilder sat in the second to back pew, but he could tell they were off their feed. He led several songs: *Blessed Assurance, Come Thou Fount of Every Blessing*, and *As a Deer*. Wilder couldn't sing and felt ugly about that, but his mouth just wouldn't move. He was afraid that if he opened his mouth his heart would burst out and fall on the floor.

Clarence led a Bible study from the back of the first pew, like how he had preached on Sunday morning. The text was from Deuteronomy 15, about the animal sacrifices in the temple. Everyone in attendance, men and women, chipped in with comments here and there. Everyone except Papa and Wilder.

Toward the end of the hour, Clarence casually called on Papa. "Wendell, what do you think about that? God asking the Israelites, farming and ranching people, to sacrifice their best cows and goats every year? Just kill them and go on."

Papa was surprised, but not intimidated. He thought for a second, needing some time to catch up. Like Wilder, his body was in church, but not his mind.

"Well, Clarence . . . I don't know. I've never had to do that. It seems a hard thing to ask of somebody."

"Would you kill your best bull, with 100 years of improved genetics, if you thought God asked you to? The text says, 'thou shalt pour his blood out on the ground as water.'"

"I don't know. It would be a lot harder than just writing a check." Papa said this kindly, not as a challenge. "Could you do it?"

Clarence paused and pinched his bottom lip, staring off at the airy wood framed ceiling with mud dauber nests in the corners. He closed his heavy leather-bound Bible and hitched it up to his side and stood up.

"I don't know either. But that is the crux of it isn't it? Faith isn't about words, very often."

That ended the study and a few more songs were led. The Lord's Supper was passed for any that might have missed the morning service. Everyone knew the gesture was meant for Papa, since everyone in attendance that evening had been there that morning as well. Papa took his grape juice and matzo bread as Wilder just watched, having not been baptized yet.

When the service concluded Wilder slipped quietly outside. It probably seemed rude, but he couldn't bear having to talk to anyone. He sat on the sidewalk around the side as the sun began to ease down. A large flower bed was covered in deep purple irises. They had bright yellow tongues that looked like they were shooting out of some kind of dragon mouth. They were nice, and he absent-mindedly wondered how long they would bloom over the summer.

In a few minutes Clarence appeared around the corner and tousled his hair ... again. Wilder stood up and nodded to the man. Clarence gave him a deep knowing smile. Wilder's eyes watered, and he knew that Papa had told him. He felt the flood in his heart spilling and it hurt so bad.

"Wilder, there was a man one time that had thousands of horses and cows. He was wealthy in land and money and everything else, and everybody wanted to be like him. He had barns and pastures and live water everywhere. He had everything he ever wanted."

Wilder listened.

"But in truth he never really owned a one of those animals. He thought he did. But he had never lost a single one."

Wilder was looking down now, quietly crying. Clarence put a hand on his shoulder and leaned down to look into his eyes. He knew what Wilder was going through, what all men go through eventually who raise livestock.

"To own a horse—to really own and understand them—you have to lose one."

That night Wilder made no entry in his journal.

CHAPTER FOURTEEN

Talking in the Dark

Wilder woke up with a headache the next morning as sunshine streamed in his bedroom window. He hadn't slept well. He dreamed that the Spanish Peaks, the two mountains he could see from his house in Cottonwood, had caught fire and burned down. He saw horses and cows up in the tall pine trees like birds. They were on fire just like the rock and snow of the mountain. Now awake, he knew that didn't make any sense, but he had been terrified in the dream.

He was starving, having eaten almost nothing the day before, and it was that need that he saw to first. Marisol had come and gone quietly yesterday, although he had seen her car in front of the house. He ate cinnamon rolls, which he knew had been brought just for him, and two chorizo and egg burritos.

Papa was somewhere in the house. He could tell when he went outside and saw the pickup parked in front. Wilder sucked in a deep breath

and walked out to the pens, which he knew
held his horse. He saw another horse close to
the corrals.

It was Fancy, leaning over the barbed-wire
fence of the Upton pasture, which connected
to the pens. She was 50 yards away from Bluebonnet's body in the center corral, but she
pointed straight to him and whinnied and dug
at the pasture beneath her with her front feet.
Her body was tensed and glistened from a light
sweat. Her eyes locked on the dead colt's body.

When Wilder got close to Bluebonnet he
saw immediately that something had gnawed
on part of his horse's hind quarter during the
night. Coyotes, he assumed, had snuck up to
the pens and broken the hide open a little. He
didn't cry, but he felt a rage at the cruelty of
the act. He knew that when animals die there
was no funeral, no burial in a nice flowered
place. They were simply hauled off somewhere
in the pasture and the myriad of insects and
animals that were designed to take care of the
dead would do their business.

But today that fact felt ugly and mean. That
wasn't going to happen to his horse.

He went to the barn and opened the big
front door. He found a shovel mostly worn out
with a hole in the middle. He saw numerous
thick steel chains but after handling three of

them to find an appropriate length, left them as they seemed too coarse for the job he was going to attempt.

In the tack room there was a stack of fuzzy old calf ropes, probably all with twists in the loop from too many stretched calves. They were past their roping use and Wilder grabbed two.

In a belligerent mood he walked straight to Papa's pickup and threw the shovel and ropes on the flatbed and started the diesel without getting permission. He put the pickup in gear and opened a series of gates to fit the pickup into the corral where his horse lay. Fancy watched and stomped her feet.

Not looking for Papa, but with a single-minded purpose, he backed the pickup into the corral. He bumped a post on the gate and heard it crack. He could fix it later. He looped the calf ropes around the lifeless back feet of Bluebonnet and tied off to the trailer ball. He patted Bluebonnet on the head and said "Sorry, boy." He climbed into the truck again and dragged the horse out into the grass trap. He didn't notice Papa watching from the front porch.

The procession of diesel pickup and dead horse bounced through the rough pasture as Wilder wandered side to side looking over the dash for a good spot. He saw the plum thicket where he and Bluebonnet had first played their hide and seek game, and chose it as the place. He stopped where the horse would rest right at the foot of the small trees.

Fancy had followed the pickup along the fence in the other pasture and now stood across from him, looking into the grass trap over the plum thicket and barbed-wire fence that separated them. Wilder turned off the engine and got the shovel, unhooking Bluebonnet from the ropes. He knew that people spoke at funerals, and so he took out his tally book journal and read the first three entries, but then had to stop when he got to his poem. He figured God and Bluebonnet knew he tried.

Near his horse's head, he started to dig.

Wilder's mind couldn't grasp the Herculean effort it would take to properly bury a 900-pound animal with just a shovel, but that detail would have been irrelevant even if he had. He was happy, in that way, that he now had something he could *do*.

He couldn't go back and make sure the gate was closed. He couldn't go back and shut the barn door after talking to his mom Saturday night. He couldn't tell Papa to put away the poisoned oats. He couldn't save Bluebonnet. But he could make sure that coyotes wouldn't get to tear his horse to shreds all over the pasture.

His shovel bit the dirt again and again, and

the soft sandy soil of the old buffalo wallow ground gave way. Huge mounds of dirt flipped up and out of the beginning hole like a badger digging a gopher out. It was easy digging, and soon Wilder had to stand in the hole to take fresh shovelfuls. He figured he would be done by lunch. A sweat formed on his brow and was absorbed and wicked away by his felt hat.

Wilder heard quail all around him as he worked. The bobwhites called back and forth on the ranch with their "bob-white" whistled scream. There were no clouds in the sky and the sun's rays seemed to be showing up faster than normal Wilder thought. He stopped and leaned on his shovel. Cicadas began their heat song.

It hadn't rained since he had arrived at the ranch, so he was about 18 inches down before any moisture could be seen in the dirt, turning it from light tan to mealy red. Wilder dug and flipped the red dirt, which now was falling back into his hole. He was an hour into the project and sat down on the edge realizing he was going to have to refigure this job. His hole was only about three feet deep and not half as long as the horse that lay before him. He was going to have to move the dirt he excavated much further away than he had been throwing it, to prevent it from falling back in.

He realized that the horse was about four feet wide lying down on its side. A hole deep enough to prevent coyotes and coons from digging and eating on the horse would need to be six or seven feet deep. And then there were the legs to reckon with. There wasn't much to them, but they now stuck out straight and were stiff as boards.

Wilder had a headache and needed water, and maybe an aspirin or two. He looked at his hands, which had already developed several small blisters. They were on each hand where he gripped the shovel the tightest.

Wilder stopped, sighed, and looked over at Bluebonnet. He saw that the colt's eyes were dry now. A thin layer of dust rested on them, and it seemed mean that the top eyelid wouldn't blink and freshen the dark black eyes. As Wilder leaned on the knot that his hands made on the end of the shovel and which pressed against his heart, the ugliness of death seeped into him for the first time. Staring at the dead eye, he saw something flutter and land from the corner of his.

He looked and saw a large butterfly was resting on the edge of the open wound that the coyotes had made on the right flank of the horse. Wilder had tried not to look too closely at the torn red flesh this morning, but now his eyes couldn't look away. He turned and focused on the bug.

The butterfly was drinking.

It was an orange and yellow monarch, trimmed with fuzzy white dots on black matte. Wilder eased down to observe the strange sight more closely. Squatting on his knees in the fresh grave, he watched, inches away from the butterfly. The monarch was drinking from the oozing damp of the wound; a hurt that would never heal. It flexed its wings open . . . shut, open . . . shut, several times while its hair-thin proboscis probed the wet pool of fluids under it.

Again, open . . . shut, open . . . shut, the big wings moved like butterfly breaths. Proboscis probing like a straw in a large soup bowl.

The color and the aroma of the wound had attracted the migrating butterfly just as a flower would. The wound was a flower, Wilder thought, the only flower that a drought could produce. In a drought you get what you can get. That is the way it is in droughts. The butterfly pulled life-giving nutrients from the dead and bloodied animal that had so tragically come to lay before it.

Wilder didn't know butterflies fed on anything but flowers. It seemed strange, but somehow, it also pleased him. He didn't scare it away. He watched until the butterfly had its fill and then flapped its wings in big floppy Monarch beats and rose into open air and skittered back and forth through the pasture and finally from sight.

It seemed like a girl butterfly, Wilder thought. And he wished he could go too. Just fly away.

But finally he knew he had to ignore the blisters and the butterflies and throw himself back into the job. He used his deep reserves of anger, both at himself and the coyotes, and his natural stubbornness. He knew how to work and not give up, and he could finish this.

After another hour of digging, the hole was bigger but Wilder's whole body ached. His head pounded in the withering sun, and his hands were now bleeding. The largest blisters had swelled and popped and he tried not to let go of the shovel even when he rested because the blood and the clear blister fluid had dried to the shovel handle, and ripping his hands off hurt even worse. His back throbbed.

There was a little mountain range of red dirt all around the hole except for where Bluebonnet lay. It took a deliberate and careful effort now to steady each shovelful of dirt and heave it over the top of the dirt piles and make sure it landed on the backside of the mountain and stayed out. He only accomplished this about half the time. The hole and the heat and the misery of it all were beating him. He lay down in the hole, receiving partial shade from the 11 o'clock sun and enjoying the rich smell of the moist dirt. He gripped the wet sand with his wounded hands, and it felt cool and good.

He felt like crying, but he was too tired to cry. And then he fell asleep.

An hour later Papa packed some lunch and drove the other truck, the ancient red Ford F-150 feed pickup, out to the pasture. He was pretty sure what was going on, both the grave-digging and the exhaustion and blisters. He had let the boy go, knowing it was good, even though it was going to be difficult.

He was surprised to find him gone when he got there. The little scene at the plum thicket was strange. Wilder had moved a considerable amount of dirt, he thought. As he pulled to a stop, he saw a small flock of wild turkeys in the plums, picking and eating the ripe plums that had been hit by the brief hail storm in May. The curious birds saw the feed truck and stormed off, making little "put-put" sounds back and forth as they retreated and vanished into the thick bunch grass and cedars.

Papa sat there in the pickup, still kicking

himself mentally at his stupidity in causing this mess. The feed pickup had a petrified buffalo bone in the ashtray that Livy had found when she was little. It had ridden a million, it seemed, ranch road miles bouncing in that little spot near the stick shift. He picked it up and held it in his brown sun-spotted right hand. "I blew it this time, little girl," he said out loud.

The words woke Wilder, and he sat up straight in the hole and peered over the edge. "Hi, Papa," he said, still dazed at what was going on. He had been sleeping deeply for 45 minutes as the turkeys picked the plums all around him.

"Oh, there you are," Papa replied, not feigning his surprise. He got out of the pickup and walked up to the scene as Wilder dusted himself off and climbed out. Papa handed him a Dr. Pepper. It was in a glass bottle and had the old 10, 2, 4 logo on it. Papa also handed him a bottle opener. Wilder had used one once and figured it out after several tries. The Dr. Pepper was cold, but it was old. It tasted flat like Dr. Pepper syrup, but Wilder said thanks, and the sugar and caffeine seemed to sink into his bones and revive him.

"I came to help, if you'll have me," Papa offered, but respecting Wilder's space and decision to take on such an enormous but noble task. "Let's eat lunch first."

Wilder nodded, answering both the lunch and the help invitations. Papa had a hot bowl of carne guisada and a sack filled with tortillas. He set them on the flatbed of the pickup and handed Wilder a plate and a fork. They filled plates, and Papa lugged a half-frozen plastic milk jug full of brown sun tea. They walked to the nearest cottonwood tree and sat down in the shaded grass and leaned their backs against the tree and ate in silence. Wilder was ravenous. He ate two platefuls. Papa noticed his hands, how shredded they were.

The tree they sat under was a young female. Papa could tell it was a female by the small green catkins that were releasing their fertilized seeds to the air in small puffs of cotton. When he stood up he picked two large heart-shaped leaves from the tree and placed one inside his hat and handed the other to Wilder. Wilder knew what to do with it, feeling good that it would keep him cool. Or at least the thought of it would help a little with the heat.

The food now gone, they returned to the hole and Papa grabbed the shovel he had brought with him. Wilder's hands had crusted over and swelled around the blisters into an angry red color. The dried blood was black.

Papa saw that he was having a hard time gripping the shovel while the wounds broke open afresh.

"Well, that was ignorant," Papa said to him straight.

Wilder looked up pitifully at his granddad. Didn't he have any compassion in him? he thought. He was trying the best he could. He wanted to lash out and say something mean, like how it was sort of his fault too that they were even out here. Like why did he have to be so mean and cold all the time? But he held his tongue.

"Put some purpose in your grief," Papa said and handed him a pair of work gloves from his back pocket. Wilder pulled them on slowly, carefully. They fit close enough and were a relief.

"It's not wrong to be sad about this deal, but you still have to think before you do things. I have dug many graves."

They worked past mutual exhaustion and through three shovels that mercifully broke and provided ample excuse to go to the barn and fetch replacements—and take a break— though they were finally forced to repair one shovel with a heavy steel pipe, which clumsy but better than nothing. Papa said they just had to keep going. One shovelful after the next. That was all. You can't get all the dirt at once.

Keep going.

They were so quiet in their work that the turkeys came back on the way to their evening roost and picked a few plums within a football's throw of them. Side by side they dug and rested and dug and rested, and the gallon tea jug worked its way down to empty and was replaced twice. They worked through second and third winds and into the place where your body feels like a hallucination, moving but seeming separate from your soul. Wilder had never felt that before. Papa had. The sweat soaked through their grey felt hats and layered new darkened stains that grew above their hatbands like storm clouds at evening. They didn't quit until the job was done, which was after dark, and even then they sat late, neither wanting to leave the holy place it seemed they had entered, together.

Sitting there in the dark, Papa told Wilder a story he would remember for the rest of his life. It was a story about a duck and a coyote.

CHAPTER FIFTEEN

Calluses

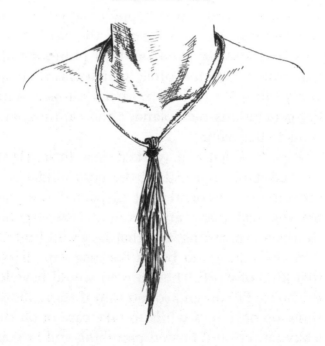

Livy and Molly and Hank drove down later in the week to pick up Wilder and they stayed a few days. Wilder was happy to see them. He and Molly swam every day in the stock tank. Livy and Molly picked sandhill plums (Molly fed most of hers to Coffee, which was no help) and made jelly in her mother's kitchen with her generations-old colander and canning jars. It made her happy.

Papa brooded and worked very little. Hank worked hard; he repaired the post Wilder had broken in the corral and inspected the gate his son had made and thought it was good. He fixed everything else that he could find all over the house and barns because Papa hated that kind of work. The old man would have let the house fall down around him if Hank didn't show up once in a while to take care of all the leaky faucets and busted plumbing and broken windows and rotted boards.

Wilder and Molly rode Fancy. Molly loved it. She braided the mane and tail on the friendly mare, but Wilder couldn't enjoy it. He loved Fancy, but he felt the guilt of losing Bluebonnet and the lack of a challenge in riding a broke horse. Fancy could still move fast and work cattle all day, but she was trained . . . she was predictable. Wilder felt that urge, the way Tequito had as a boy, to challenge himself with young horses. He knew someday he would work them again. Despite the sorrow, the rush of taking a raw colt and making it into something useful was in his blood now.

Wilder spent a day in the machine shed banging around, and everybody left him alone. When he came out that evening he had a wooden tombstone under his arm. It was a thick gray board about two feet wide and five feet long and rounded at the top. Wilder had stained it with several coats of leftover wood sealer so it looked dark and fresh. With a router he had written deeply in the dry wood:

BLUEBONNET
potro bien

He walked out to the burial site and dug a hole, wincing at the pain in his hands, and placed the board in it so that the top stuck out about three feet. Wilder was surprised that he felt more anger than sadness as he did it.

Molly walked out behind him intending to help but stayed back and watched from under a hackberry tree.

The Goods said goodbye to Papa and drove back to Cottonwood, and no one spoke much, at least not to Wilder, about Bluebonnet and the fresh mound of dirt in the grass trap. Papa had smiled when they left, but it took a visit from his buddy Red to get him going again.

Wilder kept the blood-stained gloves.

That summer all he did was climb into his treehouse and read. He was reading *The Odyssey* by Homer, in small bites savoring it, and thinking he needed to take a big trip, alone. He wrote a few poems too. He worked on one titled *Lament for a Bluebonnet*, but he was never satisfied with it, as nothing seemed good enough. He would show it to his English teacher, Mrs. Brann, when school started, he thought. He never got together with his best friend, Big, which was unusual, even though Big had called a couple of times.

Nothing seemed to interest him, not to mention that his hands were in various states of bloody bandages from the digging. It was hard for him to grab anything really hard.

Livy climbed up to his roost one day on

the hand-made rope ladder, which was risky for the frail woman. She told her son she was worried about him. Wilder told her that he felt like he lost his heart. She said that was OK.

She said that love always comes back to you. Always.

Then she kissed the top of his head like she had when he was a little boy and climbed back down the rope ladder. Wilder watched her from the trapdoor.

Toward the end of July Wilder was high in his treehouse as usual. It was in the backyard cottonwood that towered over a dry creek bed. Molly came running out and stood next to the massive tree, looking up at Wilder. He had the rope ladder pulled up.

"Wilder, Sunny is here!"

"What?" his eyes opened in shock as he looked over the edge of the rail.

"You heard me. She's here."

"Why?"

"I don't know. Are you just going to sit up there?"

Wilder put a fresh green cottonwood leaf in his book as a marker and laid it down. He threw the ladder into the trap door opening and worked his way down.

In the front yard, Livy and Josephine, the moms, stood talking. Sunny was on her knees loving on Huck. Huck was on his back receiving it all with rapid tail whaps and a dog smile that Labs do best. Sunny fingered the v-gap in his ear where the black bear they had met on their fishing trip had forever notched him.

She had wildflowers in her hair. And she was wearing braces.

The wildflowers were white and yellow daisies that made a crown around her blond hair that was loose now and on her shoulders, unbridled from her usual braids. He knew the flowers had been put there for him. And he knew he wouldn't mention them.

She looked up and Wilder smiled back at her, but then she blushed and forced her mouth straight to hide the braces. She had never done that before. Wilder thought she was the prettiest thing he had ever seen.

"Hey, Wilder."

"Hey, Sunny," he said as he walked over to her. She stood up, and Huck flipped up and ran a big circle around the lawn, ripping the turf as he went. They hadn't seen each other since the fishing trip when Gale had been hurt at the beginning of the summer. Wilder didn't know how to explain it, but seeing her now, he felt a bond with her. It wasn't just his childish feelings of thinking she was pretty; he felt connected to her now. Kind of like a sister, but different. The struggle of that night by the river had changed them both. At least he thought he saw the same thing in her eyes when she said hi.

The two made small talk, kind of in shock at seeing each other in the summer, and it being at Wilder's house. Their moms went inside, talking nonstop about school and kids and plum jelly recipes. Molly and Wilder and Sunny walked to the backyard, and Wilder showed Sunny around to his chickens and trails and his treehouse. They didn't go up, but he told her all about it.

Molly went inside to get them some ice water and the two kids sat on the back deck. Sunny didn't know how long they would be alone, so she took the chance to bring up his horse. "I know about Bluebonnet. I am so sorry."

The comment surprised Wilder, but he felt glad to have her mention it.

"How do you know?"

"Moms talk."

"Oh . . . I guess so." He thought, "It was my fault."

"I got your letter, and I was going to write back. But that next week my mom told me what happened and I didn't know what to say. So I didn't say anything."

"Well, there was nothing for you to say. It

happened and you just have to go on. That's what Papa said. Said I was entire." Papa had said a lot more, Wilder thought.

"What does that mean? Entire."

"I don't know. He said I had to figure it out."

Sunny nodded and squinted at the mountains that rose on the horizon behind the house.

"I bet you will," she said, turning and looking at him.

"My kid horse died several years ago, Scarlett," Sunny said. "She just got old and was lying there in the pasture one day. I'll never forget how weird it was to see her lying there. Just like that."

"At least it wasn't your fault."

Sunny felt his wound and understood it, but she didn't respond to it.

"Are your hands healed up?" she asked.

"You even know about that?"

"Moms talk. Everybody knows about it I guess."

Wilder showed her his hands. The blisters had healed slowly and were now faint red disks in several places, covered with peeling white rings of dead skin. They didn't hurt any more, not much. The blister spots were thick calluses now. His hands were useful again, but they were changed.

"My dad says you are a cowboy now. Now

you understand horses and life and death. He said burying a horse by hand is magnanimous."

"Papa dug half of it."

"Still."

"What does magnanimous mean?"

"I think it means great."

They sat and mulled over magnanimous in silence. Sunny saw a small lock of braided black hair peeking out of the top of Wilder's shirt connected to a leather strap. It made a loose necklace around his skinny neck. It looked kind of like a turkey beard, a short one.

"Since when do you wear a necklace, Wilder?" Sunny pointed and laughed.

Wilder leaned back and stuffed it down, embarrassed.

"It's not a necklace. It's a medicine bag—or the beginnings of one. Indians had them."

"What is it?"

"A piece of Bluebonnet's mane, but I'm not supposed to tell you that. It's supposed to be a secret. I might lose the medicine."

"Ohh," Sunny said, in reverence now.

"I need to keep it close."

Sunny scratched her nose by stretching her mouth open and wiggling her top lip like a rabbit does. She was the only person Wilder knew who ever did that.

"I made up an Indian name for you this

summer," she said as she stood up. They both heard Josephine holler through the back screen door that it was time to go.

"Oh really?"

"Yeah. You're Boy-with-Big-Medicine."

Wilder liked it.

The day before school started in August Wilder received a package in the mail. It was a medium-sized box that had come from Mexico: Piedra Amarilla, in the state of Jalisco— Wilder read the address and saw the strange looking stamps. He unwrapped the box slowly. Inside was a thick set of oily off-white rawhide coils wrapped in Mexican newspapers. It was a hand-braided 55-foot reata. There was a note in the middle that read in Spanish script:

Wilder, muy vaquero
— Teq

THE END

ᘁ

ABOUT THE AUTHOR

S. J. Dahlstrom lives and writes in West Texas with his wife and children. A fifth-generation Texan, S. J. has spent his life "bouncing around" the countryside from New Mexico and Texas, north to Colorado and Montana, and east to Michigan and New York. He is interested in all things outdoors and creative. He writes poetry and hunts deer; he plants wildflowers and breaks horses; he reads Ernest Hemingway and Emily Dickinson and C. S. Lewis and Søren Kierkegaard.

S. J.'s writing draws on his experiences as a cowboy, husband, father—and as a founder of the Whetstone Boys Ranch in Mountain View, Missouri. He says, "I wrote this story about Wilder Good for kids who grew up in the outdoors and for kids who long for the outdoors ... working, fishing, hunting; farms, ranches, mountains and prairies. I think all kids want to do these things and go to these places." The Adventures of Wilder Good is his first book series.

You can learn more about S. J. Dahlstrom and join Wilder Good on his adventures when you visit the Wilder Good website, *www.WilderGood.com*, where S. J. encourages readers to 'Be Wilder' and submit photos and stories about their own adventures.

Coming Soon!

#5

THE ADVENTURES OF WILDER GOOD

BLACK ROCK BROTHERS